MW00480023

JOY OF MY HEART

ROMANCE FROM THE HEART BOOK 3

LEE TOBIN MCCLAIN

Ask and you will receive, and your joy will be complete.

— JOHN 16:24

1

Lucas Ruiz Morales hadn't expected a big brass band to greet him, but having someone at least answer the door would have been nice.

He tapped again on the door of his ancestral home in Arcadia Valley, Idaho. Yes, his grandfather had been sick, but where was Connie, the housekeeper? Where were the visiting nurses?

After repeated knocking, Lucas retrieved the key from the spot under a decorative planter where it had always been kept and let himself into the house. Maybe his abuelo was asleep. Lots of older people lost some hearing. Maybe he just hadn't heard the knocking.

He was ashamed he didn't know more about his grandfather's condition. But that was all about to change.

"Belo?" He walked through the sprawling home that his parents, both now gone, had fondly called La Hacienda. He stepped in the master bedroom to find tangled bedclothes, pill bottles on the nightstand, and a large-print library book open, face down beside the pillows.

The man himself was nowhere in sight.

"Belo?" He called louder now and checked the adjoining bathroom. Empty.

His footsteps echoed as he hurried to the big farmhouse kitchen. It was a lonely sound, and guilt stabbed him again. For his grandfather to be rattling around by himself in this giant place wasn't right. Yes, Lucas had arranged for nursing staff to be there around the clock, but that didn't make up for the lack of family.

And speaking of nurses, where were they? And where was Amiga, Belo's beloved, three-legged corgi mix?

"Hello? Belo? Anyone?" He called louder now, searching the dining room and living area.

He heard a thump.

Lucas cocked his head, seeking the source of the sound. He heard it again. From the basement.

"Belo?" Surely his grandfather couldn't make it down the old house's steep cellar stairs. The man was almost ninety.

But when he checked, a dim light shone from the basement, and there was another thumping sound.

Bracing himself for intruders—because maybe he'd missed a memo and Belo was staying somewhere else, leaving an opportunity for thieves to break in—Lucas made his way down the stairs, hand on the sheathed knife in his pocket. He wasn't a violent man, but you didn't spend a decade as a war correspondent in the most remote, dangerous parts of the world without learning to take care of yourself.

He reached the bottom of the stairs and a shape rose out of the darkness. He lifted his knife and feinted left, then moved right, and some kind of stick came crashing down where he'd been.

He caught his assailant around the waist.

A small, bony waist. With a familiar, musty-spicy smell. "Belo?"

"So, you have finally arrived," Belo said in his precise, accented English. "Why are you creeping up on me?"

"I thought you had an intruder! Didn't you hear me calling?" He loosened his grip and eased his grandfather over toward the steps. "What are you doing down here, anyway?"

"I am searching out something for you." The old man gestured toward a pile of boxes. He'd obviously been down here awhile, going through them.

His wrinkled hand was ice-cold. Not good. "I can get you whatever you need later," Lucas said. "Come on upstairs."

"Not until I find it." Belo stumped over toward the pile of boxes. "It is in here somewhere. I remember."

"What are you looking for?"

"Mama's necklace." His legs wobbled as he lowered to his knees and rifled through a box in the dim light. "Make yourself of some use. That blue box—right there—pull it down. You are as tall as a giraffe."

The grumpy words made Lucas grin, but he obediently reached up and pulled down the box his five-foot-six grandfather couldn't possibly have reached. "If you'll tell me what it looks like, I'll help you find it. Is it in a jewelry box?"

"Pouch. Velvet." Belo shoved aside the box he'd been working on and opened the one Lucas had gotten down for him. "Green, I think."

Lucas turned on the flashlight from his phone and shone it into the box. Immediately, he saw a scrap of green velvet. "Is this it?" he asked, extracting it from the heap of papers, ribbons, and china knickknacks.

"At last you have done something useful. Help me up."

That was Belo. If you wanted a bunch of easy compliments, you didn't turn to him. Lucas extended his hand and helped his grandfather to his feet, steadied him, and then shoved the boxes out of the middle of the floor with his foot. "Satisfied now? Can we go upstairs?"

Belo didn't answer, he just led the way. Which was good, because Lucas wanted to walk behind to catch him if he fell.

The old man made it up the stairs, slow step by slow step, and shuffled to the kitchen table, sinking into a chair with a little groan. "Ah, Miho. I'm not as young as I used to be."

Tell me something I don't know. "Where are your nurses?"

"I did not like them," Belo said, "and they did not like me."

Lucas could only imagine.

"So I sent the last one away yesterday. Because you were coming."

Oh, man.

Lucas wasn't sure how long he could stay. His new work as a freelance food-and-health writer wasn't exactly location dependent, but since his assistant was in New York, he based his travels from there.

As if on auto-pilot, he moved to the old stove and put the kettle on, just as he'd watched his grandmother do so often in the past. He opened and closed cupboard doors, looking for tea, noting with dismay the sticky film on some of the dishes and the lack of supplies. Why were the cupboards so bare? He could barely find a teabag.

"So what happened with Connie?" They could start there. Belo's housekeeper had worked here for most of her life and she'd never have left the kitchen in this state.

Belo shrugged. "She had to go take care of her sister. I'm fine. Get these worthless nurses to do a little work."

"But... they can't keep up if you've fired them." Lucas opened the refrigerator, which held a carton of milk—expired—a few wilted celery stalks and peppers, and a package of lunch meat. No wonder Belo was getting so thin.

"It doesn't matter. Sit down." Belo's voice was still authoritative, and Lucas was still enough of an obedient grandson that he obeyed.

"I want to talk to you. Give you something." He held up the green velvet pouch with shaking hands and fumbled to open it.

Lucas wanted to grab it away and do it himself, but respect compelled him to let Belo take his time.

Finally, he got the pouch open and extracted a tarnished silver necklace, embedded with turquoise and rose quartz. "Ah, still beautiful." He held it out. "This is for you."

Lucas took it and studied it. "It's a women's necklace. I remember Mama wearing it."

"That's right." Belo nodded. "And now, it is time you found a woman to give it to."

Lucas lifted an eyebrow. "What do you know about women in my life?"

"Only that you don't have them," Belo said with a disgusted snort. "Not enough, anyway. Not one special one."

That was undeniably true, and there was a good reason for it. Lucas stood and went to the stove, checking the gas burner and listening to the water start to boil. "Where's the mutt?" he asked, seeking to change the subject.

"I lost her two months ago." Belo's voice thickened, just a little, and Lucas glanced over and saw the sadness on his grandfather's face.

How lonely the old man must be without his loyal companion.

But Belo wasn't one to share the softer emotions. He cleared his throat. "There is something I want you to do."

"Oh? What's that?" Lucas was getting a bad feeling. He poured the water over teabags in two cups, even though it wasn't quite boiling. He carried the cups to the table.

Belo put his hands around the outside of the cup but didn't drink it "The time has come for you to marry."

"Oh, really?" Lucas frowned, dunking his teabag. "Why's that?"

"The Ruiz name dies with you and me," Belo said, "unless we continue it." He flashed a ghost of a smile. "And I haven't met anyone lately."

The weak attempt at a joke, more than anything else, made Lucas sit up and take notice. Belo wasn't usually much for joking. "What brought this on?" he asked, buying himself time to figure out how to tell Belo what he needed to tell him.

Belo reached out a veined, wrinkled hand and gripped Lucas's forearm with surprising strength. "I have a diagnosis."

A hollow feeling started in Lucas's stomach. "What is it?"

"It's my heart, complications from the diabetes," Belo said. "The odds aren't good."

The hollowness spread to Lucas's chest and throat, making it hard to breathe. He put his hand over Belo's and looked down at it. Two brown hands, one old, one young. Both with the thick fingers and prominent veins of a Ruiz.

They were the last of their line. Could it be true that Belo wasn't long for this world?

No. He didn't accept that. "What doctor told you that?" he asked. "There's nobody here in Arcadia Valley qualified to make that kind of diagnosis."

"The doctors sent me to Twin Falls," he said. "There, I was seen by good doctors."

"Good local doctors, sure." Lucas blew out a sharp breath, his head filling with plans. "We'll set up an appointment at the Carnegie Clinic in Denver. I have a friend I can call—"

"You are not listening." Belo clutched Lucas's arm tighter. "I don't need a big-city doctor. What the Twin Falls Heart Center said was good enough for me, nothing less than what I've sensed myself."

"But Belo—"

"I'm eighty-nine years old, and I have had a good life. But this conversation isn't about me." He took up the pendant Lucas had put down and handed it to him again. "I want you to marry and have children. It's time. Before I go, I want to see you settled down here on La Hacienda with a good woman. Preferably pregnant."

Lucas stared at his grandfather. Had the old man lost his mind? "I have a few plans other than finding and impregnating a wife," he said. "Something called a career?"

Belo waved a dismissive hand. "You can write books anywhere. And it does not take so long to find a woman. Why, I met your grandma—"

"I know, at a VA dance, and you married her a month later," Lucas said. He'd heard the story a dozen times.

"And we had a happy life," Belo said. "My one regret is that we only had one child." He looked away, but not before Lucas saw reflected in his eyes the same pain that was in Lucas's heart. His parents. Happy and in love and doing good work one day, dead in a car crash the next, victims of a drunk driver.

"So carrying on the family name is up to you, and you're not getting any younger. What are you, thirty?"

"Thirty six." Thanks for the reminder.

"*No hay mucho tiempo*. You must find a woman. Polish the necklace before you give it to her." Belo pushed back his chair and stood. "Now, I must go to bed. You make yourself at home, and I'll see you tomorrow."

Was this some kind of a joke? "I'm not getting married, Belo."

His grandfather opened his mouth to speak and then closed it. His eyes were more watery than Lucas remembered.

Then his grandfather shook his head a little and turned away. "I am tired," he said as he headed toward the door. Frailer, maybe even shorter than he'd used to be.

Lucas stared after him, shaking his head. The old man was *loco*. People didn't get married to continue a family name, not anymore.

But that didn't make Lucas feel any better about disappointing him.

FROM THE HOSTESS stand of El Corazon, Veronica Quintana smiled at the McKennas, parents of a classmate she'd known her whole life. "Thanks for coming in tonight," she said, her friendly customer service persona coming back to her, as comfortable as an old pair of jeans.

She'd loved her writing job in Twin Falls—well, most things about it—but, reluctant as she was to admit it, El Corazon was home.

Mrs. McKenna shrugged into the coat her husband held for her. "We adore Mexican food! But it's too bad about your job, honey."

"Thought you were running the website for that big newspaper over in Twin Falls," Mr. McKenna boomed, loud enough for the half-full restaurant to hear. "That gig sure didn't last long!"

The smile froze on Veronica's face. "No, it didn't." Three months, to be exact.

Three months of being her own independent woman, until things had gone terribly downhill terribly fast and she'd come home to Arcadia Valley with her tail between her legs.

And while she loved El Corazon, she didn't love the feeling of failure that reared up whenever people asked—or didn't ask, but obviously wanted to—about what had happened to the new job.

"Well, we're glad you're back." Mrs. McKenna patted Veronica's shoulder. "It's always nice when our young people stay in

Arcadia Valley. And with your family here to take care of you, you can take your time figuring out your next move."

"Or maybe there won't be a next move," Mr. McKenna said. "Nothing wrong with helping out in the family business. Your parents would be glad."

Veronica glanced automatically at the large portrait of her parents on the restaurant's wall. They'd started this place, had loved it, had made it grow. They'd both been excellent cooks with a good sense of what customers wanted.

Whereas Veronica couldn't fry an egg without burning it.

As the couple left the restaurant, Veronica's oldest brother, Javier, strode out of the kitchen and toward the hostess stand. "Heard you got home late last night," he said as he picked up the clipboard to see which tables were still available. "Where were you?" His eyes scanned the restaurant, checking everything out, making sure there wasn't a napkin or fork out of place.

"Yeah, where were you?" her brother Alex called from the other side of the dining room. He wore a white apron and was bussing a table, subbing for an employee who'd called in sick.

She glared at Alex. He was just a couple of years older than she was and should know better than to stick his nose into her business. He was supposed to be on her side against their oldest brother's overprotectiveness.

"It's okay." Her middle brother, Daniel, spoke up from the table where he sat with his twins and his new wife, Tabitha. "She was at Karaoke night at the American Legion. One of my patients mentioned it." He tilted his head to one side as he looked at Veronica. "Did you really sing 'All My Exes Live In Texas?' Twice?"

"I love that song," one of the few remaining customers said, and started to whistle it.

Veronica let her head sink into her hands.

She was twenty-six years old, with a college degree in media and journalism. She'd lived on her own, hosted exchange students, helped to start a women's prayer group. When she'd moved to Twin Falls, she'd made new friends right away. She'd started volunteering at an animal rescue farm and singing in the church choir.

And then everything had blown up around her. Her confidence had been shaken, her sense of herself as a professional—and as a woman—chopped down.

And now here she was, back in Arcadia Valley, living with her brother and his wife. And having her every movement scrutinized by not just Javier, but her two other brothers and half the rest of the town as well.

She had to get out of here. To lick her wounds, to regain her self-assurance, to start over.

"You boys leave Veronica alone." Tabitha put an arm around her. "She's a grown woman, and it's nobody's business what she sings at the Legion!" She lifted an eyebrow at Veronica. "Although I wish you had better taste. Country music... ugh."

Alex slipped over and changed the music station from Latin contemporary to wailing country. When Tabitha glared at him, he laughed. "Just want to bother my newest sister-in-law."

"Veronica will always be my baby sister," Javier said. "And I don't like the idea of you staying late at the Legion, *hermanita*. Most of the folks there are good people, but you never know—"

"Thanks for your concern." She was going for sarcasm, but it fell flat.

Because the truth was, as much as she railed against it, a part of her *did* like her brothers' concern. Wasn't that why she'd come running back to Arcadia Valley?

"Come on, let's have some girl talk." Tabitha pulled Veronica out of her seat. "The rush is over, and your brothers can handle whoever's left."

Veronica followed her friend to a corner table, grabbing a

basket of chips and a cup of salsa from the stand beside the kitchen. "Is it just me, or are they ridiculously overprotective?"

"It's not just you." Tabitha laughed. "Daniel's the least overbearing, but even he can get bossy when it's a question of family. But they mean well."

"They do. I know they do. It's just... I got a taste of freedom living in Twin Falls. When I came back, everything felt different." She sighed. "Seems like they didn't grate on me as much before."

"Well, you weren't living with Javier and Molly before," Tabitha said. "Living at the cottages gave you at least a little bit of freedom. Do you want to come stay with Daniel and me and the girls?"

Veronica crunched a chip. "You're sweet. But I'm not going to be a third wheel with you newlyweds."

Tabitha snorted, looking over at the table where Daniel was wiping up a drink one of the twins had spilled. "It's not like we have a lot of privacy anyway, with the twins around."

Daniel glanced over their way, and when he noticed Tabitha looking at him, his lips turned up at the corners.

Their gazes locked, and it seemed to Veronica that the temperature in the dining room went up by ten degrees.

"Daddy! Can we have flan for dessert?" one of the twins asked. Daniel got involved in that discussion, and Tabitha looked back at Veronica, a faraway look in her eyes and a smile lingering on her lips. "What were we... oh. Yeah. You'd totally be welcome to stay with us. We'd love to have you."

That was all she needed, to watch Tabitha and Daniel fall ever more deeply in love when she'd ruled that out for herself. "Thanks, but no. What I need is my own place."

At least, until she could scrape together the money to leave Arcadia Valley.

"You can't get your cottage back?"

Veronica shook her head. "No. Those places are in high demand, since there aren't many rental properties around." She sighed. "I feel like I'm going backward in my life, you know? All I want is to stand on my own two feet and be independent."

"I hear you," Tabitha said sympathetically. And she wasn't faking sympathy, but Veronica couldn't miss the way her eyes flickered toward Daniel again.

All three of her brothers had found love in the past two years. They'd all settled down and were living their adult lives.

Only Veronica still wandered, acting like a kid, staying out and singing Karaoke. Which, for the record, hadn't even been that much fun, since she'd been one of the few sober customers in the place.

The bells on the front doors jingled. "That's my cue," she said to Tabitha. She walked up to the hostess stand, glancing at the clock on the wall. Eight forty-five, so the kitchen was open for another fifteen minutes. And it had been drilled into her by her parents: treat the last customer just as well as you'd treat the first. "One for dinner?" she asked, picking up the menu.

Only then did she look closely at the customer. Hair cropped as close as a military man, brown eyes, muscles to die for. He was familiar, and yet not.

"Take out," the man said. Then he did a double take. "Veronica? Veronica Quintana?"

From three separate points in the room, her brothers' dark heads swiveled toward the newcomer.

"I'm Veronica." She studied him, trying to keep an impassive expression as her insides jumped and danced. "Do we know each other?"

2

L ucas stared at the beauty in front of him. And then tried
   not to.

"Lucas Ruiz Morales!" A hearty voice boomed out, and then
Javier Quintana was pounding him on the back. "When did you
get into town?"

"¿*Qué onda*?" called one of the younger Quintana brothers—
Alex?—from across the room. "Long time no see."

"Hey, Lucas." That greeting came from Daniel Quintana, the
genius of the family, who was there with a pair of adorable
twins.

Okay, so the Quintana kids were all here and accounted for,
albeit a lot more adult than they'd been the last time he'd visited
Arcadia Valley and seen them. "Your parents?" he asked, keeping
his eyes on Veronica.

"Both gone," she said.

"I'm sorry." He meant it. The Quintanas had been fixtures at
El Corazon, and in Arcadia Valley, for as long as he could
remember.

"Thanks. How's your grandpa? I heard he was having some
health issues."

"Our abuela keeps us in tune with the gossip," Javier said, a friendly hand still on Lucas's shoulder. "Is he doing okay?"

Lucas shrugged. "Not the best, but he's hanging in there." Guilt tugged at him. If everyone in town knew how badly Belo was doing, then it was worse than he'd thought.

And arranging for nursing care from afar wasn't enough. Not nearly enough.

"Are you here for awhile?" Veronica asked.

If you're going to be around, he wanted to quip. Thankfully, he didn't say it aloud.

Although, from the way Javier's hand tightened on his arm, he might have let some of what he was feeling show.

Which he shouldn't. He'd meant it when he'd told Belo that he didn't intend to marry. And Veronica Quintana was the kind of girl you married, not the kind you toyed with. Not if you wanted to live out the rest of your life in one piece, given her brothers, who were now all circling around him.

"I don't know how long I'll be staying," he admitted. He was still marveling over Veronica, whom he'd encountered a few times when he was home from college. Then, she'd had braces and acne and been shy with everyone. Now... she was a woman.

A very pretty woman.

"Come sit," Javier said, and urged him to a corner table. Alex joined them and after a minute, Veronica came, too.

Daniel stopped by the table and introduced his family, the twins and his wife, a pretty brunette. "I'd like to stay and catch up," he said, "but I have some sleepy little ones." He put a hand on each twin's head, and then the four of them headed out.

"He seems happy," Lucas commented. "And El Corazon is looking good. Lots of updates. I'm surprised." The restaurant had always been an important part of Arcadia Valley, but a little outdated, more for his parents' generation than for young people. Now, though, the décor was colorful and modern, and the specials listed on a chalkboard included vegan tacos and something called "locally-sourced enchiladas frescas."

"It's a lot to do with my wife," Javier said. "She redesigns restaurants for a living. She helped El Corazon move into the twenty-first century."

"And now, we have a lot more business," Alex said. "But you're used to a lot bigger city than Arcadia Valley, right? Didn't I hear you were living somewhere overseas?"

Lucas nodded. "Copenhagen, then Prague. Before that, the Middle East. But I've been back stateside for a couple of years, living in Pittsburgh."

"I heard Pittsburgh is hopping. Lots of nightlife," Veronica said. "I'm envious. It must have been fun."

He laughed a little, shook his head. "You'd be disappointed in me. I work all the time."

Especially given that his personal life had pretty much gone down the tubes.

But he didn't want to think about that. Deliberately, he sat back and drew in a deep breath, let it out slowly. A simple relaxation technique and it worked.

It also made him hungry, given the fragrance of grilled meat and onions and homemade *masa* tortillas.

"I liked your last book," Javier said. "You working on another?"

"Just getting started, looking around for the right subject," he said. "Poking at some research, but I've been too busy with speaking and the like to settle on anything."

"You should write about Arcadia Valley," Alex suggested. "You do health and food and all that, right?"

Lucas nodded.

"Arcadia Valley has changed a lot. Organic foods, green living, sustainability. It's a whole different place from where you grew up."

"Is that so." Lucas had gotten a lot more interested in food and health in the past few years, for obvious reasons. "Maybe I'll look around while I'm here. I wouldn't mind staying, especially with my grandfather being ill, but I'm a bit stuck without my assistant. She handles the website and speaker requests and helps me with research."

"Couldn't she come to Idaho?" Alex asked the question. Even though he'd been a major league baseball player, he still saw Arcadia Valley as the center of the universe, one of the most desirable places a person could go.

Lucas shook his head. "Doubtful. She's a city girl. We have plenty of room for her—there's that guest house in back of our main house—but she'd consider this the middle of nowhere."

"You should think about settling down," Alex said. "This is a good place for it. I'm 100% happier since I came back here to stay."

Javier punched his arm. "Patricia might have something to do with that."

So young Alex was married, too, or at least attached. Interesting. The Quintana brothers had settled down.

Nowadays, Lucas could see the appeal of that. He'd spent too much time globe-trotting to make a success of relationships. Regret pushed down on him. He'd made too many mistakes.

"Is there a girlfriend?" Javier asked him.

"Is the assistant the girlfriend?" Alex wiggled his eyebrows up and down in a comic way.

"Nope." He glanced at Veronica as he said it, but she was looking at her phone, ignoring the conversation.

"So you work all the time and don't have a girlfriend," Alex said. "You *do* need to come home. Remember how to live!"

"Oh, that's Arcadia Valley, all right," Veronica said, glancing back up from the phone and tuning into the conversation. "Nightlife galore."

"If any of us knows, she does," Alex said. "She's the queen of the American Legion, these days."

"The Legion, huh?" Funny, he wouldn't have pictured Veronica as the type to hang out with a drinking crowd.

"She's the only one without responsibilities," Javier added.

Some emotion Lucas couldn't read crossed Veronica's face. "That's me, no strings," she said lightly.

Interesting. "Maybe you'll show me around sometime."

At that, Javier, Alex, and Veronica all stared at him, and he realized he'd sounded like he was trying to make a move.

Maybe he had been.

Whether he was or he wasn't, she didn't take the bait.

TWO DAYS LATER, Veronica stretched out on the living room couch at Javier's house, capped her bottle of Passionate Pink nail polish, and frowned out at the rain.

"Hey, check it out," Javier's wife Molly said from the other couch, holding up her phone. She, her daughter Trina, and Veronica were doing their nails and watching an old movie, whiling away a Sunday afternoon. "That guy Lucas Ruiz who just moved back to town? He's advertising for a research assistant and secretary."

"Can I apply?" Trina looked up eagerly. Just fourteen, she was searching desperately for a summer job.

"I don't think so, honey." Molly reached out and rubbed Trina's back. "He wants an adult, someone experienced at research and with websites and social media."

"Hello, I'm almost in high school," Trina said, rolling her eyes. "We write research papers practically every month. And I'm online all the time."

"He wants an adult," Molly said. "He's offering a place to live in."

"Who's that?" Javier came into the room, wearing flannel warmup pants and a U of Idaho T-shirt, his face dark with stubble.

"Your buddy Lucas. He's advertising for an assistant." Molly held up her phone for him to see.

He scanned it. "Guess his New York assistant didn't want to move," he said. Then he glared over his reading glasses at Veronica. "Even though it fits your qualifications, I don't want you applying for it."

Veronica had thought a lot about Lucas since they'd seen him, but she had absolutely no interest in going to work for one of her brother's friends who was older, Latino, and undoubtedly just as domineering as her brothers were. Still, Javier's remark put her back up. "Why?"

"I didn't like how he looked at you."

Two blond heads spun to face Javier. "How'd he look at her?" Trina asked.

"Wait, isn't he your age?" Molly asked Javier.

"Like, *old*?" Trina added, grinning.

Veronica snickered. It was awesome that Javier had a teenager comfortable enough with him to tease like that. He'd adopted Trina when he'd married her mom just a couple of months ago, cementing a relationship that was already strong.

Javier put his hands on his hips and pointed a mock-scolding finger at Trina. "One, he's not old, but he *is* older than me. Which means he shouldn't have been looking at my sister like she was..." He broke off at a frown from Molly. "That way," he concluded weakly.

Molly lifted an eyebrow at Veronica. "Any interest on your side?" The corner of her mouth lifted.

"No," Veronica said. "No way. I have enough bossy men in my life."

"But if she took this job," Trina said, "then you could rehire Aunt Mariana."

All the adults froze. Trina looked around uneasily. "I guess I wasn't supposed to say that," she said.

Veronica felt a little dizzy. "Wait a minute," she said to Javier. "You fired Mariana to hire me?"

Javier scraped a hand across his jaw. "Not *fired*," he said. "Laid off, more like."

"Raquel says she's bummed out." Trina shrugged.

"Trina! Mariana is fine," Molly snapped. "If anything, she's enjoying the chance to put in a garden and do some spring cleaning."

"Wait," Veronica said, staring at Molly, whom she considered a close friend. "You knew he did this and you didn't tell me?"

"And money's not a problem," Javier added, ignoring her question. "Don't worry. You know family comes first. You needed the help right now, and Mariana didn't."

Veronica's heart pounded faster and her face heated. "So did you kick someone out of the guest room to have me live here, too?"

"No!" Molly came over and sat beside her and put an arm around her. "It's not like that at all. We're glad to have you. We *love* having you here."

"We really do," Trina added. "Don't be mad, Aunt Veronica."

Veronica stood. "It's okay, honey," she said, patting Trina's shoulder. "I'm not mad. At *you*." She strode out of the room, stopping beside Javier. "You, you're another story," she said.

"Now, Ronnie..."

"Pet names don't mean you can treat me like a pet!" Out in the hall, she pulled out her cell phone, found the job ad Molly had shown her, and punched in the number.

Lucas answered, his low voice making Veronica's stomach tingle.

She ignored the feeling. "Hello, this is Veronica Quintana. I'm interested in the job you advertised on the Valley Bulletin site."

"BELO, for the last time, I'm not in the market for a wife!" It was Monday morning, way too early for this. Lucas straightened his grandfather's bedclothes and then picked up the tray of mostly uneaten breakfast food and set it on the dresser.

He was tempted to overturn the sloshing cereal bowl on his grandfather's head.

"I'm telling you, you should be." Belo tried to sit up and groaned. "You're not as good looking as you used to be, when you had more hair. But surely there's someone out there who would overlook a few flaws."

"You're just ragging me." Lucas ran a hand over his closely shaven head. "This is the style." He gripped Belo under his arms to help him to a higher, more comfortable position in the bed. When he felt his grandfather's bony ribs, worry gripped him. "We need to focus on getting you well. When's your next doctor's appointment?"

Belo waved a hand. "Monday, Tuesday, I don't know."

Lucas picked up one of the pill bottles on his grandfather's nightstand. "Dr. Currie? I'll give him—her?—a call and check the time."

Belo blew out a disgusted breath. "He is too young to know anything. I don't want to go. All they will do is tell me there's nothing they can do."

That didn't sound right. Lucas studied the pill bottle more closely. "Belo, this is expired. *And* the bottle's full."

"I don't trust it. All the chemicals."

"But... it's to help your diabetes." Lucas picked up another bottle. "And this one's for your heart. It's full, too."

"Connie was supposed to bring me some tea for that," Belo said. "I like the old ways better."

"Tea?" Lucas stared at his grandfather. Belo wanted to treat his complex heart issues with tea?

"Yes, tea. With the healing herbs. Now, let's talk about you. What have you done to meet a woman you can settle down with?"

Lucas sank down onto the side of his grandfather's bed. "No wonder you're not feeling well. You're ignoring your doctors' advice."

"You're ignoring my advice to hurry up and provide me with a grandson." Belo glared at him.

"First of all, you'd have a 50-50 chance of getting a grand-daughter, not a grandson." Lucas picked up some tissues and a magazine that had fallen to the floor. "This place is a mess. When is Connie coming back?"

"You could keep trying. Have many children!'"

"You're changing the subject." Man, the air was stale in here. He walked over to the window and opened it.

"No, *you're* changing the subject."

They glared at each other.

"You won't be here long, anyway," Belo said with a shrug.

Lucas breathed in the dry, high-desert air, scented with sage. He'd tried to get away, but he had never forgotten this place, all that it offered. He'd never been able to escape the feeling that this was home. Being back here, seeing all the familiar people, being with Belo, held an undeniable rightness.

He made a decision, one that had been cooking in his mind for months. "I'm here for the long run. I'm staying."

Belo tilted his head to one side, his eyes narrowing as if he were trying to read Lucas's sincerity.

There was a light tap on the door. "Hello?" came an uncertain female voice.

Lucas turned around as awareness danced up his spine. "Veronica!"

"I'm so sorry to walk in. I knocked, and rang the bell..."

"One minute." He turned away from her and back to his grandfather, to check on him but also to get his own reactions under control. Veronica was wearing slim-fitting black pants and boots, with something loose and flowery on top, her hair tumbling over her shoulders. She was prettier than any woman had a right to be.

"That bell hasn't worked in a year," Belo said. "Who is it?"

"I'm interviewing an assistant." Lucas raked his fingers through his hair. "Are you okay for now?"

"*Si,* I am okay." Belo frowned irritably at him. "I have been managing for many years without you. Cooking me breakfast once does not make you my guardian. I'm not that old yet."

Lucas raised his hands like stop signs and backed out of the room. "Sorry. You're right." Disrespect was one thing Belo wouldn't tolerate, and Lucas didn't blame him.

He turned and strode out into the hall where Veronica stood, obviously close enough to hear everything that had been said. "Come on, this way." He led the way from the bedroom wing to the dining room, which he was using as an office.

He wasn't prepared for this interview. He was worried about Belo, for one thing. He'd been running around waiting on the old man since he'd gotten up, and as a result, rather than feeling prepared and professional, he felt frazzled, his back and neck tight with tension.

This was just a courtesy interview, anyway. No way could he hire Veronica Quintana for a live-in position.

She was pretty and charismatic and all too tempting. He couldn't take the risk.

Besides which, her brothers would skin him alive if he hired their sister. They'd as much as ordered him to stay away.

"Have a seat." He gestured toward the chair and moved behind the desk where he had his laptop and files. He spent a moment sifting through papers, trying to collect himself.

He hadn't had any other applications for the position, and his files were already showing the lack of organization. His emails were piling up. He needed help.

"Did you want to look at my resume?" she asked after a moment. There was a question in her voice, but no worry.

She'd matured into a poised professional. A lot more poised than he was, at least today.

"Of course. Of course, I will." He held out his hand and took the nicely-formatted document Good college grades, an internship, and a couple of good post-college positions, his businesslike side noted. "But why don't you tell me a little bit about why you want the job. I thought you were all set at El Corazon?"

"No." She shook her head. "Actually, that job was temporary, so now I'm looking for something else."

"This job is temporary, too," he said, latching onto the excuse. "If you're looking for something more permanent—"

"I'm not," she interrupted. "I just need to earn some extra money while I figure out my next move."

He wanted to know her next move. He wanted to hear where she'd been and why she was leaving. But he had no right to know, no reason. It wasn't his business in the least.

He frowned. "The pay I'm offering isn't spectacular. The deal-sweetener was the live-in accommodations, but I'm sure you'd want to live at home with your family."

"*Au contraire*," she said drily. "I need a place to live."

Lucas's stomach turned over. Worse and worse. "You want to live here? What will your brothers say?"

She gave him an icy smile. "If they say anything, the answer is that it's not their business."

He swallowed, not wanting the image of Veronica Quintana

living on the estate to lodge itself in his brain. He set aside the question of what her brothers would say, for now. For now, but not forever. "The job is a bit of a mishmash," he said, looking for more excuses not to hire her. "It's technology and PR and research, all the stuff I mentioned in the ad. But it's also some basic secretarial work, getting me organized. And on top of that, it turns out there will be some caregiving for my grandfather, too." There. That ought to turn her off.

She shrugged. "I'm trained in the research and tech skills, not in caregiving," she said. "But I've helped with my abuela when she was sick. Old people like me."

Of course they did. Everyone probably liked Veronica, especially men.

With a sense of doom he scrolled her through his website, pointing out areas he wanted to improve. Then he pulled up a massive research list and printed it, figuring it would discourage her. Gestured at his messy desk and showed her his 576 unanswered emails.

No such luck. In fact her eyes it up. "I can totally look into this stuff."

"Let me show you around." He had to get out of this small room with her. He was having trouble thinking straight.

He walked her through the kitchen, the front rooms, the gardens, dwelling on the inconveniences and rushing her through the gorgeous spots.

She seemed unfazed.

Then he walked her toward Belo's room. "Belo?" he asked, tapping lightly.

Belo was dressed now, lopsidedly, and sitting on the edge of the bed. "And who might this be?" he asked, his face transformed by his broad smile.

Veronica stepped forward before Lucas could introduce her. "I'm Veronica Quintana." She grasped Belo's hand. "We've met, but it's been awhile. I'm Isadora Quintana's grand-daughter."

"Ah, Isadora.... " Belo looked at Lucas. "I knew you could do something right." Is this the girl you're hiring, or... have you finally decided to listen to me?"

"About what?" Veronica asked, looking at Lucas.

If Belo said he was trying to find a wife for Lucas, Lucas would personally strangle him.

Apparently, his glare conveyed some part of his feelings to Belo. "I fired all my caregivers," he said to Veronica. "But Lucas has his hands full. If you can help him a little bit around the house as well as the office, he'd be grateful, I'm sure." This was said in Belo's rapid Spanish.

She replied in Spanish as well. "I'd be honored, Señor."

"Wait a minute, Belo. Veronica hasn't agreed to take the job." And he hadn't offered it to her.

Didn't want to offer it to her.

"I'd be very glad to work for you," she said, "if you'll give me a try."

The words created all sorts of images in Lucas's brain. But with two pairs of brown eyes looking at him, with either longing or mischief in them, he wasn't sure which, he was helpless.

"I'm going to need to call Javier," he said, "to see what he thinks of the whole idea."

Veronica put her hands on her hips and glared. "You'll do no such thing."

"But he's the head of your family," Lucas said, and glanced over at Belo, who nodded. "If he's against my hiring you, I can't do it. He's an old friend."

A world of emotions swirled in her eyes. "Look, Lucas, either you hire me on my own merits or you look for someone else. I'm not waiting for you men to negotiate over me like I'm a peace-weaver from Anglo Saxon times."

She was right. He shouldn't do any such thing.

"Then... we're stuck," he said. "Unless...."

She lifted an eyebrow.

"Unless you'd agree to help me with one project. I want to interview a doctor at the local hospital. I'm going to do it while my grandfather's at a support group. If you'd like to do some preliminary research and take notes for me, we could test the waters that way."

"Perfect," she said immediately. "Just show me what you want me to do."

"I have another appointment," he said as a sense of impending disaster crashed down on him. "I'll send you some research questions, instructions and the schedule we're looking at. But remember, it's just a trial run."

OKAY, so a trial run, Veronica thought the next day as she pulled into the parking lot at the hospital. She'd talk more to Lucas today—she hadn't yet moved in—and just see how this job was going to work out. If it was great, she'd commit. If not, she could stay at Javier's and El Corazon, no harm done.

Except that she'd seen the danger of letting herself stay under the thumb of dominant men, even her own brothers. She'd made a major mistake and very nearly gotten herself into a very bad situation.

She got out of her car, laptop tucked under her arm, and stood in the parking lot waiting for Lucas to arrive. Which he did, just a moment after the arranged time. He pulled into the space adjacent hers and got out of the car, hurrying around to his grandfather's side with a quick wave to her.

He helped his grandfather out of the car, one arm under his elbow and the other hand holding a cane. Belo—she'd already started calling him that—frowned and snapped, but Lucas ignored the moodiness and didn't move away, but rather handed the old man his cane and took a step back, watching carefully, ready to assist.

Her own brothers were nurturing, but she'd rarely seen that quality in men outside her family. It softened her heart toward Lucas.

Once they were steady, she walked over and joined them as they headed into the hospital, arguing.

"I don't want to be in a support group," Belo grumbled. "I don't need support. I have you."

"It takes a village, Belo," Lucas said, a trace of humor in his voice. "I don't know anything about diabetes, and the people at the hospital do. Let's give it a chance, okay?"

As they crossed the lobby, Veronica saw a couple of nurses she knew. One of them looked at Lucas, nudged the other, and they whispered and laughed a little.

It didn't seem Lucas noticed, but she sure did. Her arm itched to slip across his shoulders and claim him as her own.

Whoa, she told herself. Don't even *think* about falling for him, because that would lock you into staying into Arcadia Valley forever. Staying small. Submissive. Not being your own person. And with a man who's way too much like your brothers.

They walked into the room where about twelve chairs were arranged in a circle. Grey-haired members of the group were finding their seats while others milled around, probably family members and nursing staff.

Then she heard a familiar, beloved voice. "I have to come to the hospital to see my own *nieta?*"

"Abuela!" Veronica spun, delighted, and hurried to her grandmother. She folded her into a careful embrace, then helped her into her seat. "I didn't know you came to this group."

"There are plenty of things you don't know about me," Abuela said tartly. Then she looked up and saw Lucas and his grandfather, and an expression of shock crossed her face. "Is that Benito Ruiz?" she asked.

Veronica nodded. "I'm going to be helping his grandson with some research." For some reason, she didn't feel like telling her grandmother it might turn into a full time job. A full time, *live in* job.

"Watch yourself. Those Ruiz men are..." She glanced over at her friend. Who, as old and wrinkled as Abuela was, smiled and nodded.

Abuela said something quick and quiet, that Veronica couldn't catch.

So what was the reputation of the Ruiz men, and did it really go back generations?

If so, it was even more reason for Veronica to be careful.

"If everyone would find your seat," a scrub-clad nurse said, "we'll get started. We have a real treat today: cancer survivor Beatriz Soler is here to tell her story about how healthy eating helped to put her cancer into remission."

Lucas was stepping back from his grandfather, but at the words from the front of the room, an electrified expression crossed his face.

Veronica wondered what that was about as she hugged Mama Beatriz, a member of her prayer group.

Lucas pulled out his own laptop and beckoned to her. "Do you know the speaker?"

Veronica nodded. "She's a good friend."

"Let's sit and listen to her talk," he said, "and maybe you could use your connections to help me get an interview with her later."

"Of course, but what about talking to Dr. Jones?"

"Later," He waved a hand. "Right now, we might learn something here. This is an area I might explore in my new book."

So they sat and listened to Mama Beatriz talk about growing

chemical-free vegetables, eating a plant-based diet, and focusing her prayers on gratitude. Veronica knew the story already, but she was still moved by the way this wonderful woman had outpaced what amounted to a death sentence.

After the talk was over, Javier came to get Abuela. "Some of the members are coming to lunch at El Corazon," he said to Veronica. "Everyone is invited, actually, so we might get a bit of a crowd."

Veronica glanced over at Lucas. "Want to go?"

She expected him to say no, but he didn't. "If you don't mind my changing plans midstream—which you'll have to get used to if you work for me—we'll get to our interview later," he said. "Interviews, actually, because I'd like to meet Beatriz, too, and hear more about her journey. But for now, I'd like to take grandfather to lunch with the group. He needs to get out more."

"I'm not going to a Quintana restaurant," Belo said.

Abuela had been walking out with Javier, but her hearing was still very sharp and she obviously overheard Belo's remark. She turned back. "Scared?" she taunted.

"Quiet, woman," he said. Then he beckoned to a nurse. "Get me the doctor."

"Still haven't learned your manners, eh?" Abuela said.

"Still haven't learned yours?" he retorted.

They glared at each other, and Veronica glanced at Lucas. He looked as confused as she was.

"Manners aren't about submitting to men," Abuela murmured, her cheeks flushed.

Veronica hadn't noticed her grandmother taking this type of attitude toward anyone before, so when Lucas and his grandfather were safely in the hallway, headed toward the car, she asked her about it. "What is Señor Ruiz to you?"

Abuela snorted. "He *wanted* to be something to me," she

said, "but only if I would take the proper women's role. Which to him, meant silence."

Veronica lifted an eyebrow. "The more things change, the more they stay the same."

"And that is why I chose your grandfather instead," she said, "even though that man had his share of *charisma*." She stared in the direction of the door through which Belo had departed.

The interest in her eyes suggested that she hadn't entirely gotten over Belo. Either that, or he'd rekindled her interest today.

Okay. This was interesting.

"Chica, it's good to see you," said another of Abuela's friends, embracing Veronica. "I saw you talking with Lucas Ruiz."

Veronica nodded. "I'm doing some—"

"It would be nice if you had someone like Lucas to take care of you," the woman interrupted, "since you aren't going to be a journalist."

There was so much wrong with that statement that Veronica couldn't even answer. But Abuela did. "She doesn't need someone to take care of her." She took Veronica's arm. "She is perfectly capable to care for herself."

But the older woman's words made Veronica frown. She'd better be careful about having fun with Lucas, working for him, thinking about him. Maybe she shouldn't do the job. Because if his presence made her feel less independent, he was a definite danger to her plans to leave Arcadia Valley.

BELO GOT INVOLVED in a conversation with an old fishing buddy, giving Lucas time to observe Veronica. She'd gone back to talking with her grandmother, apparently saying goodbye.

He watched the way she leaned down to talk to her grand-mother, then came around to the front of her chair, taking her hands. She spoke respectfully, a smile on her face, and her abuela flashed a matching smile almost instantly.

Just seeing their relationship made Lucas happy. He'd tried dating women from other cultures, but they didn't always share the same family values.

When Javier wheeled their grandmother away, Lucas beckoned Veronica over.

"I don't think I should do the job," she said the moment she got within earshot.

Emotions washed over him, upset and anger and relief. But mostly, hurt pride. "Why not?"

"Lucas Ruiz!"

Lucas turned to see the doctor he'd been seeing since arriving in Arcadia Valley. "I hope everything's okay? You're not sick again, are you?"

Lucas tried to telegraph "Patient Confidentiality" with his eyes. Quickly, he introduced Veronica. "We're here to interview people. Veronica is... may be... helping me with my research for my medical book."

"Hey, Veronica!" The doctor looked at her, his eyes warm. "Are you thinking of shifting your career toward medical writing?"

She tilted her head to one side. "I haven't figured that out, to be honest."

"Well, you should consider it. That would be such a great path to any kind of a job you want. Medical researchers and writers are in short supply."

"That's the first I heard of it," she said. "I thought nothing I could do, as a journalism and media major, was in short supply."

"Are you kidding? We science types are horrible at writing and we don't have time to research. If you get this experience and can show it, you can write your own ticket."

They continued chatting while Lucas tried to rein himself in and think about his writing project.

Today's speaker had definitely excited him. He'd felt that sharp tang in his throat, that frisson up the back of his neck, that told him he was onto something. Paying attention to that kind of intuition was a key to his success.

He looked around the corridor, thinking. Busy, uniformed people hurried by. Voices chimed around them, a mix of Spanish and English.

He looked around at the shiny floors, listened to the quiet voices making announcements and the "ping" of the elevator.

The hospital smell made him flash back on frightening times, and he felt a twinge of misgiving about the potential new direction of his research. He liked to do work with a personal connection, knew it made him a better writer, but there was such a thing as too personal.

The doctor's pager went off. "Got to go. Nice to see you both."

When the doctor was gone, Lucas looked at Veronica and saw conflict on her face. "What's wrong?"

She shrugged. "Look, Lucas," she said, "there are some... family issues I guess... that might make it hard for me to work for you."

That was curious. He shrugged, pretending indifference. "It's okay. I can put out the ad again."

"No." She put a hand on his arm and warmth radiated from the spot where their skin made contact. She must have felt it, too, because she pulled her hand back and bit her lip.

"No, what?" He couldn't keep his voice steady unless he lowered it. She was a beautiful woman, and kind, too. He'd seen her with her abuela, as well as with her nieces, and he knew she was a caring person.

If he'd been in the market for a woman, she might well have

been it. The type of spicy, talk-back female that raised his blood pressure in a good way.

But he wasn't in the market. Couldn't be in the market.

He'd spent way too much time in hospitals. They held memories of pain and suffering and fear of death.

What he'd gone through had changed him. Yes, in some ways he wouldn't have chosen, but also in ways that made him understand what was important and see the value of home and family.

He couldn't change the fact that he'd neglected his grandfather and the homestead for the past ten years. And he didn't dare to get close to a woman again.

But he could change what he did going forward, so that when he was as old as Belo—if, God willing, he was blessed enough to reach that age—he didn't have regrets.

One of his jobs would be to stay with Belo, take care of him. The other was to use his God-given abilities to write a book that would help others.

The topic of that book had gotten clearer today, and the hospital reminded him that time wasn't unlimited.

So he'd commit, then. He would commit to the book, and get Veronica's help if she were willing.

If not, he'd find someone else. He could do it. Veronica might be extremely attractive, talented, and similar in values, but that didn't mean she was irreplaceable as an assistant.

"No," she said, "don't put the ad out again. If you still need me, I want the job."

"Live in?" he asked.

She bit her lip again and nodded.

"Good." He nodded too. "I did talk to Javier, and—"

"You talked to Javier?" Her eyes flashed dark fire.

"Yes, and he wasn't happy about it, but he didn't absolutely forbid it. Your living on the property would be helpful to me because I tend to work strange hours."

"It would be helpful to *me*," she muttered, "because I wouldn't have to live with my bossy brother anymore." She studied Lucas speculatively. "Although..." She trailed off.

He took a step closer, drawn to her, and lifted an eyebrow. "What?"

"I may be jumping out of the frying pan into the fire."

3

That Sunday afternoon, Veronica turned her car into the Ruiz-Morales homestead. Her heart began beating faster.

"You can always back out," Molly said from the back seat. "I wish you would. I'm going to miss you staying with us."

"But this is a great opportunity for her," Tabitha argued from the passenger seat. "Doing research for a well-known writer, running his PR side and social media... it's exactly what Veronica trained for. Didn't you have a dual major in journalism and media?"

"Uh-huh." Veronica let her sisters-in-law argue as she pulled her car in front of the little cabin where she was to stay.

"It's cute." Tabitha climbed out and put the seat forward for Molly.

"It's tiny." Molly crinkled her nose. "You'd have had more room staying at our house."

"Yeah," Veronica said, "but there's no big brother here to boss me around and try to run my life."

"Don't be too sure." Molly nodded sideways, and Veronica looked to see Lucas, now striding out from the main house. He was big and purposeful and way too handsome. "I think Lucas might be cut from the same cloth as your brothers."

"Only bigger," Tabitha whispered. "I think he's taller and..."

"Brawnier?" Veronica asked. She was going for a dry, humorous tone, but the word came out breathless instead. Lucas had a couple of inches on Javier and Daniel, she was pretty sure, and he had shoulders and arms of a weight lifter.

"Hello, ladies," he said as he approached. "I'll let you in and show you around. It should be clean and ready to go."

But when they went inside, there was a bedroll on the floor and an opened can of soup on the counter. A coffeepot on the stove was still warm.

"What on—" Lucas broke off and turned toward the three women. "Go back outside," he ordered. "Stick together and near your car."

"Bossy," Veronica murmured as she followed her sisters-in-law out the cabin door. She didn't feel afraid. If someone had been using the cabin to crash in, maybe that was a sign that she shouldn't move in. She was ambivalent about the job and the living situation, which she'd taken in a fit of pique. Javier's spare room, while annoying, was safe, and she was surrounded by family. Out here, she'd be alone with Lucas and his grandfather.

And some hobo, apparently.

Sharp male voices rang inside, and then Lucas came out, pulling a scruffy boy by the shoulder. "He won't tell me who he is," he said. "Anyone know him?"

Molly did a double take. "Terrance? I thought you were living out of state."

"Terrance is my brother. He's a year older than me. I'm Tyrone," the boy sighed. "Let me guess: you hate Terrance because he did something awful to you."

Molly nodded slowly. "To my daughter."

"When Terrance got sent to military school, I got sent, too," the boy said. "But I couldn't take it and I kept running away, and now I got kicked out," the boy muttered. "Can't go home."

"How long have you been living here?" Lucas asked. "I checked this place out a couple of days ago and you weren't here then."

"Got here last night. Look, I'll leave, okay? Just don't tell anyone."

Lucas frowned. "You'll leave and go where?"

The boy shrugged, his mouth tightening. "There's got to be a place like this somewhere else."

"But how will you get food? And what about school?" Veronica shook her head. "Why can't you go home?"

"Because when they sent us to military school, they told us it was our last chance, and that we shouldn't come back."

Lucas was studying the boy, hands on hips. "Wait a minute. You look a lot like someone I know."

The boy looked off across the fields, then kicked at a rock. "You're my mom's cousin. That's why I came here. My mom's name is—"

"Salome Sarkis," Lucas broke in. "I haven't seen her since we were kids, but you look a lot like her. She kicked you out?"

Disbelief laced his words, and Veronica could almost see the thoughts going through his head. Someone from *my* family isn't taking care of her own?

The boy lifted his chin and nodded, as if to say, "What's it to you?"

"How old are you?" Tabitha asked.

"Sixteen."

Veronica glanced around at the other adults. "Too old for foster care?"

"He could emancipate if his parents agree." Lucas seemed to make a decision. "Look, we're not going to get this settled today. For the moment, I'd like to have you come inside. You can get a shower and a hot meal. And then we'll figure out what to do."

"Lucas doesn't know what he's getting into," Molly muttered to Veronica.

"Gather up your things and I'll help you carry them into the house. Ladies, if need be I can get a cleaning service out here."

"We can clean up," Molly said. "But I'd like to talk to you for a minute."

"She's gonna tell you I'm trouble." The boy sounded resigned.

"Would I be lying?" Molly asked.

Tyrone shook his head. "Nah. I made plenty of mistakes. Though I'd never have done what Terrance did, if it makes a difference. I leave younger girls alone." He drew himself up and faced Molly. "I apologize for my brother."

His earnest expression touched Veronica's heart. She remembered the night that Molly's daughter Trina had gone missing. She'd snuck off with Terrance and he'd ended up trying to take advantage of her, but fortunately, scrappy Trina had managed to defend herself until Molly and Javier had found her.

"You're not responsible for what your brother did." Molly shook his hand.

"Come inside for now," Lucas said to the boy and then turned to Veronica. "I was going to show you around, but there's nothing much to show. Do you mind...?"

"No problem." Veronica's heart went out to Tyrone, who stood slumped. He was just Trina's age, but while she was a confident child, this boy looked like a jaded old man. And the fact that his family didn't want him broke her heart.

She would see what she could do for the boy. But Lucas had it under control now, so she'd let it be.

Inside, they made quick work of cleaning up the slight mess the boy had left.

"The place is cute," Molly admitted. "I like the little sleeping loft, and the kitchen nook is cozy."

"Get your furniture in here, and it'll be just like home."

Pine-paneled walls and a plank floor. Best, a little built-in book case and a gas fireplace. She could make this a home. And it would be a home of her own, one she was earning with her own money, not a charity case from her brother.

The slam of a car door and male shouts from outside warned her that her brothers were arriving with the furniture. Moments later they were lifting things off the truck. Quickly, she grabbed Alex's arm and told him where she wanted everything and then went inside the big house to sign the short-term contract with Lucas.

He was talking intently to Tyrone, though, so much so that he didn't seem to hear his grandfather calling from his room. She hesitated, and then went to Belo's bedroom door and tapped. "It's Veronica," she said. "Is there anything I can do for you? Lucas is talking to someone, a guest."

"I just knocked over this tea," he grumbled. "Made a mess, and I know he hates that."

"Did you get burned? Wet?"

"I am okay, but I can't say the same for the magazines I was reading."

Veronica helped him clean up the sodden things. "What happened?"

"I was looking through my pill bottles. I have too many. Going to get rid of them." He swept them into the bedside drawer.

"Wait, don't you need to take those?" Veronica picked up a bottle that had fallen on the floor.

"No! All these fancy medications will kill me. What I need is my special tea, but I drank the last of it."

"Sit down," she urged. "Let me help you. Now, let's look at these pills. You do have a lot."

She didn't know much about medicine or health care, but as she read the instructions, she saw that they were from two different pharmacies. Also, it looked like he wasn't taking any of them, because all the bottles were full. "Do you know which of these is the most important? Which one did your doctor talk about the most?"

Reluctantly, the old man indicated one of the bottles. "That's the one he keeps harping on."

"Look," she said. "Why don't you try taking just that one, and leave the others aside? You can see if it makes you feel better or worse. Meanwhile, I'll make you some of the tea my abuela liked when she was sick. It's an old Mexican mixture and it helps with any kind of headache or dizziness."

She got him to agree, and fetched him a fresh glass of water. While he took the pill, she checked out the window and saw that her brothers were still unloading furniture into the cabin. So she found a telenovela on the TV that her abuela liked, and sat down with Belo to watch it. Soon they were both engrossed and laughing at the overly dramatic story line.

She noticed he was getting sleepy, so she helped him into bed and, after watching a little more of the show, he dozed off. She muted the television and headed downstairs. She'd fix him the tea if she could find the ingredients.

Tyrone was alone in the dining room, eating an amazing-looking plate of huevos rancheros. He looked up when she came in, but he didn't stop shoveling food into his mouth.

It must've been awhile since he'd eaten. "Did Lucas make that for you?" she asked.

He nodded and swallowed. "It's good." He looked at his plate and sighed. "I ate most of the eggs, but would you like some bread?"

Impressive that he was willing to share in his situation. "It looks good." She inhaled the aroma. "He must have heated it up for you."

He nodded and spread a slice with butter, then pushed the bread basket and butter dish toward her.

"No, that's okay." She'd had a full breakfast at Javier's this morning, and this kid needed the food more than she did. "I have to talk to Lucas."

"He's out there." The boy pointed toward the anteroom, and she heard the murmur of men's voices.

She headed toward the kitchen. She'd talk with Lucas after his company left, and meanwhile, see if she could find the ingredients for Belo's tea.

But as she walked through the hallway, a familiar voice made her stop.

"We're not happy about this live-in situation," her brother Javier said.

"We added a lock inside the door. You can charge us for any damages," Alex added, a little laughter in his voice. "I'm no pro. But." His voice went serious. "It'll hold."

There was a thump, as if Lucas, or someone, had knocked over a chair or banged something with a fist. "You didn't need to do that," Lucas said, his voice indignant. "I'm hiring her as an assistant and that's all."

Daniel made a snorting sound. "We saw how you looked at her."

"That's right," Javier added.

He'd been looking at her in some kind of a way? The thought made heat rise up inside Veronica.

The truth was, Lucas was hot. And he was a writer, her type of person. Top it off with the fact that rather than throwing a needy boy to the cops, he'd given him a meal, and he was looking better and better.

"Thing is," Alex was saying, "Veronica's never had a real boyfriend. Not since a high school crush went bad."

Great, Alex. Tell him everything embarrassing, would you?

The truth was, Alex didn't know the half of it. She'd liked Buddy McPherson, yes. She'd had a crush. And he'd laughed in her face.

And then he'd trumpeted it all around the school that they'd done things together they hadn't.

She'd gotten plenty of attention from boys, then, but not of a good kind.

It had sort of turned her off on the gender. Add on top of that experience, the whole nightmare in Twin Falls, and she was through with men.

"She's innocent," Javier said flatly. "And I want her to stay that way."

"You're too old for her anyway, Dude," Alex said.

"You'll have us to contend with if you try to make a move," Quiet Daniel added.

Javier's interference didn't surprise her, but Alex was supposed to be on *her* side. And Daniel was the gentle intellectual brother, so why was he practically threatening violence?

Veronica felt like going right in and shouting at all of them, but she had the feeling they'd just laugh at her. She'd be fulfilling their expectation that she was a silly little teenager who needed to be protected.

No. She had another idea.

Rather than yelling at them, she'd do what they didn't want her to do. She'd get involved with Lucas.

Oh, not involved, exactly. With her brothers' warnings and, she would guess, Lucas's own sense of what was appropriate, he wouldn't actually take things too far.

But it would be fun to get him to take her out on a date. He'd be a safe person with whom to practice her relationship skills. If she didn't start practicing, she'd never learn.

And contrary to what her brothers thought, she was no baby. She was twenty-six and they were right about one thing: she hadn't ever had a real boyfriend. Hadn't even dated much, aside from a few dinner-and-movies in college.

She'd never gotten deeply involved with anyone, and since she'd moved back to Idaho, she'd lived as if preparing to enter a religious order.

When in fact, God willing, she'd like to have a family one day.

But that didn't happen without making an effort. She needed to get in the game.

Before she left Arcadia Valley, she wanted to be more in the habit of dating, more aware of how to act with a man, especially a grown-up man.

And Lucas, older, honorable, and traditional, was the very man to make that effort with. Her heart leapt with the idea, and a smile curved her mouth.

This was going to be fun.

4

The next morning, Lucas tapped on the door of his grandfather's room. "Belo? You awake?" He pushed the door open, just a little.

"I'm old, of course I'm awake." Belo was sitting up in bed, with a neat tray in front of him, complete with coffee, hard rolls, butter and jelly, and a flower in a tiny vase.

"Someone's been treating you well," Lucas commented, sitting in the chair beside the bed.

"It's that new assistant of yours. She's already been in here."

"Really?" Lucas frowned. He and Veronica were going out for a full day of exploration and interviews; he didn't like it that she'd been up early, cooking and doing for his grandfather.

His grandfather beckoned him closer. "She's a looker and a sweetheart. You could do worse."

"Belo!" Lucas's face heated. "She's my employee, and she's way too young for me."

"Nothing wrong with a younger woman," he said.

Time for a change of subject. "We have a visitor, Belo. Actually, a house guest. I hope you don't mind."

Belo cocked his head. "Who?"

Quickly, Lucas explained about Tyrone, including the fact that he was a distant blood relative. "He's a teenager, and hasn't had a place to stay. I imagine he'll sleep late. But when he gets up, he's got an appointment with the local police. His school reported him missing."

"Is he going to steal the silver?" Belo asked, but surprisingly, he didn't sound upset.

"Not likely. For one thing, he doesn't have a getaway car." He sat in the chair beside his grandfather's bed. "What would you think about our having him stay awhile, if his school and his parents don't insist on having him back?"

Belo shrugged. "I wouldn't mind having the company. I've spent a few lonely years out here."

Guilt washed over Lucas. Belo had been living here alone while Lucas had been travelling the world.

Well, and healing himself, or trying to. "You don't need to feel lonely now, Belo. I'm here."

"Yes," Belo said, "but you have other things to do instead of keeping an old man company. How's the progress toward making me a bisabuela?"

Lucas looked at the ceiling and shot up a prayer for patience. "Isn't being a grandfather enough?"

"Not when there is only one son. Responsibility rests on you."

Lucas needed to nip this in the bud. "I have no interest in marriage," he said firmly. "So get that thought out of your head."

Veronica stuck her head in the door. "We have just enough time to get to our first interview," she said, looking from him to his grandfather with open curiosity.

Obviously, she'd heard what he said.

"Good, good. Keep this grandson of mine on time. He has a problem with organization."

"Thanks a lot." But Belo was right.

In fact, it was best if Veronica knew what she was dealing with. In regards to his tendency to be late and disorganized, and in regards to women and commitment, too. It was good if everyone knew where he stood.

They walked out the door, and she led the way to her car.

"Wait a minute," he said. "Let's take my car."

She shook her head. "I should drive you around. You're the famous author, and I'm the assistant."

"And I'll be bent like a pretzel in your little coupe."

"That's exactly what Javier says," she said. "Fine. Would you like me to drive your car, then?"

He opened his mouth to refuse and then caught the laughter in her eyes. She had to know that, as a man with old-fashioned values, he wanted to be the one to drive. He was every bit as traditional as her brothers.

Add to that, he was a bit of a car guy, and his current vehicle was a late model Lexus.

They both slowed down as they approached the open garage that held their two cars. And then Veronica turned to him, arms crossed and one eyebrow raised. "Well?"

"Fine." He sighed. "You drive." He tossed her the keys.

"All right!" She sounded surprised, but pleased. "This just might go okay after all."

She kept up a steady, tour-guide monologue as she drove them through Arcadia Valley, one hand on the steering wheel and the other gesturing, pointing, and waving. He had to force himself not to tell her to concentrate on her driving. But in the end, he had to admit that she drove well, and that having his own hands free made it easier for him to ask questions, take in the farms and fields, and make notes.

"First stop, Grace Greenhouse." She pulled into a parking lot. Beside the greenhouse, large gardens were tilled and planted, and Lucas could see pale green sprouts pushing through the rich soil.

Veronica introduced him to Evelyn Kujak, a high-energy woman with a cascade of brown hair, who showed him the greenhouses and talked about sustainability and vegetables and a place called Corinna's Cupboard where the greenhouse sent vegetables for donation.

By the time they left, Lucas's head was spinning with ideas.

"So what are you going to do with that information?" Veronica asked as the two of them headed back to the car. "Have you figured out the focus for your book?"

"I'm playing with several ideas. Including a book on using fresh foods for healing." He had to tread delicately here. It was obviously a subject of interest to him, personally, but he didn't want others to know. Didn't want Veronica to know, and he wasn't sure why.

"That's a great topic, and I know exactly who you should interview next," she said. "Beatriz Soler, the one who spoke to the support group. She's the mother of one of our cooks and a good friend of mine. And like she said at the hospital, she's practically healed her own cancer through sustainable living. Hang on." She veered off the highway onto the berm and pulled out her cell phone.

Lucas was busy making notes about what they'd seen, so he only paid half attention to Veronica's enthusiastic conversation. He was reeling with ideas, and his book was starting to take shape in his mind.

"Sure. We can meet you this afternoon." She lifted an eyebrow at Lucas.

He nodded.

As she ended the call with inquiries about the other woman's health, Lucas studied her covertly.

She was young, high energy, and pretty. Definitely no longer the little girl she'd seemed when he had known her last.

He could see why her brothers kept involved in her life. She must have any number of men chasing after her.

He couldn't be among that number, and it would be best if he remembered that.

The car rumbled to life. Before he could stop himself, he spoke up. "You know, you can have a social life while you're living and working with me. I'm sure you have lots of friends... boyfriends... whatever." That hadn't come out right.

She glanced over at him. "I do have lots of friends, and I go out some." She shrugged.

So, dates? Or what? Her answer had given nothing away.

"Is pizza okay for lunch?" she asked. "I'd like to take you to one of our most interesting restaurants. Aside from El Corazon, of course."

"Pizza is interesting?"

"At Fire and Brimstone it is. You'll see." She pulled into a parking lot and drove around, finally finding a parking space at the far end of the row.

She flipped back her hair as she looked over at him, and his mouth went dry.

Veronica Quintana was a bomb waiting to explode. No matter what her brothers did, she was going to be the belle of the ball if she wasn't already.

He got out, tried to go around and open her door, only to find her stepping out, laughing up at him. "Beat you," she said saucily. "You're way too much like my brothers. Always having to be the gentleman."

"Is there something wrong with that?" He took the keys from her hand and closed her door for her, then ushered her toward the restaurant—which actually looked more like an automotive garage, but whatever. With every move, he felt better, more in charge.

More like the man he was supposed to be.

Inside the crowded restaurant, they ordered their food—unique varieties of pizza that rivaled anything you could find in New York—and found a small table along the wall.

"Everything's locally sourced," Veronica explained. "So the menu changes depending on the season."

"This soda is fantastic."

"Homemade, with natural sweeteners." Veronica spoke proudly, as if she had a stake in the restaurant.

Which she did, in a way. She was proud of her hometown. And as a member of a restaurant family, she probably had a special connection to others in the same industry.

Lucas noted the vintage signs and rustic décor. A young mother herded her two little boys toward a table in the corner, waving at Veronica as she went by. Then a couple of guys in business suits stopped at their table to chat.

With Veronica, not with him, obviously. And he didn't like the way they looked at her.

She introduced him immediately—and made it clear he was her boss. Why? So they wouldn't think she was taken? Did she like one of these guys?

And why on earth did it matter to him if she did? He scolded himself, even as he made it clear to the suit guys that he didn't want them hanging around.

After they left, he realized that their table happened to be on the darker side of the restaurant. And a little too private.

"So, tell me about you," Veronica said into a silence that was starting to become awkward.

"Not much to tell. I've been writing and not having a life, as your brothers so charmingly pointed out. When I finished my last project and found out that Belo wasn't doing so well, I arranged to come home."

"That's a good thing," she said approvingly. "Family is important."

"Then why do you want to leave?"

She blinked. "How do you know I want to leave?"

"You moved to Twin Falls. And you said this job was going to be temporary. I can only assume you want to get out."

She stared down at the table, picking at a rough spot in the wood with a delicate fingernail. "I do want to leave. I've never really been on my own, and I think..." She paused.

"What do you think? You can say it."

"I love my family. I love my brothers. But they smother me. I can't really grow up while they're so close by." Her face was troubled. "I feel like a jerk for even saying that."

He put a hand over hers and then, feeling its softness and delicacy, quickly pulled his hand back. But not before she stared at him, her face even more troubled.

He cleared his throat. "I understand wanting to get away. I had the same urge when I was your age."

"That makes it sound like you're ancient." A dimple formed in her cheek.

"Not so ancient." He locked his gaze with hers.

He definitely wasn't so old that he wouldn't feel anything for a woman like her. But that wasn't a good idea because he couldn't do anything about it. And not just because her brothers would kill him. If he'd wanted to get involved with her, nothing so trivial as her family's resistance would have stopped him.

No, he had his own good reasons why he couldn't get involved. But tell that to his heart.

She was still looking into his eyes, and a slow smile formed on her face. "Why, Lucas Ruiz Morales, I think you're flirting with me."

The playful words forced an answering smile from him. "What if I were?"

She shrugged. "Like I said, I'm here for the short term. But I like to have fun."

Images of what that might mean flooded his mind for just an instant, and then he sobered. "You should be careful what you say," he said. "Some people might misinterpret."

"I didn't mean..." She blushed. "I just... all I mean is, I'm here for a short while and I wouldn't mind going out. Taking you around and showing you the sights. Nothing heavy."

That was better. "That's what I figured you meant."

She leaned forward, and this time, it was she who put a hand on his arm. "You need to lighten up, Lucas," she said. "Have some fun. You're too serious.'"

"Now who's flirting?" he accused.

"Pizza for two?" came a voice from a harassed-sounding waiter, and their pizza came down onto the table between them. Covered with roasted vegetables, it made his mouth water. "Hold that thought," he said. "I need to focus on this. Entirely."

"Not a bad idea," she said. "But keep it in mind, what I said."

THE DAY WORKING with Lucas wasn't tiring, but somehow, the emotions he evoked in her had her a little frazzled. But when Javier called her to fill in at the restaurant, she didn't hesitate. It had been drilled into her from an early age that the success of El Corazon was everyone's responsibility.

"Heard you were out to lunch with Lucas today." Javier leaned against the hostess stand, scanning the half-empty dining room. Mondays were slow at most restaurants, El Corazon included.

That was why it had seemed a little odd that Javier had asked if she would fill in as hostess. On slow nights, he or one of the waitstaff usually handled it.

"Yeah, we were at Fire and Brimstone," she said.

Javier frowned. "Is that wise?"

She shrugged, feeling uneasy, as if Javier could see right into her head. "He wants to see the town and interview people for this book he's thinking of doing. We were out and it was lunchtime. What's wrong with that?"

"Just watch out. You're already working for him and living at his guest house. You don't need to socialize with him, too."

She stared at him as realization washed over her. "You asked me to come in tonight so you could lecture me, didn't you?"

"Check on you," he corrected. "You're my baby sister, and I'm worried about you."

Indignation rose in her chest and heated her cheeks. "Javier!"

"He's a lot older and more experienced than you are." He paced and then stopped to straighten the menus. "You've been in Arcadia Valley your whole life, except when you went to college. And even that was in a small rural town."

"I lived on my own in Twin Falls!" Even as she said it, she knew it was no argument for her life experience. She'd been half an hour from Arcadia Valley, and she'd come home to visit nearly every weekend. In between, a couple of times a week, one of her brothers had stopped in to visit her.

Javier just looked at her, one eyebrow raised.

"I've been to Mexico," she said weakly.

He nodded. "With family, Ronnie. And in another small rural town."

"Which is exactly why I want to leave!' she burst out. Then she clapped a hand over her mouth. She hadn't meant to reveal that to Javier, not yet.

He leaned forward, eyebrows coming together, the corners of

his mouth turning down. "You want to leave? What does that mean?"

"I want to be my own person," she said, "and I can't, because you're smothering me!" Even as she said the words, she felt like a twelve-year-old inside. Her brothers, especially Javier, brought that out in her.

But she was twenty-six. Old enough to have a family, like her own mother had at her age. Old enough to have a big-city career, like a lot of her college friends.

Instead, here she was being lectured by her big brother for going out to lunch with a man who happened to be her employer.

"I'm only trying to protect you from Lucas." His tone was measured, like he was trying to calm a six-year-old. "Do I smother you otherwise?"

"Yes." Which was true. But it was also true that the moment Lucas had appeared in town, Javier's protectiveness had gotten much more intense. "What is it about Lucas that you don't like, anyway?"

"I like him fine," Javier said. "He's always been a good man, and he does good work. But he's hiding something."

"Really." She looked at her brother's serious face and didn't argue. There *was* something a little reserved, guarded, about Lucas. And she trusted her brother's instincts.

Around them, the dining room noises had lessened. People were paying their checks, shrugging on coats, leaving. The few who remained had finished their meals and lingered to talk and drink coffee.

"Look," she began, "I know you have my good at heart, and I appreciate—"

He put out a hand to stop her, looking at the door.

Where Lucas was coming in, with Tyrone behind him.

Javier and Veronica turned toward them. "Hey, Lucas, what's up?" Javier asked.

Instead of answering, Lucas looked at the teenager. "Go on."'

"Can I fill out a job application?" he muttered.

Javier cocked his head to one side and eyed the boy.

Veronica elbowed him. "Should I go get him one?"

It was his restaurant, of course, and she knew better than to overstep. But she also knew Lucas wouldn't have brought the kid here if he didn't think his working at El Corazon was a good idea.

"Sure," Javier said, still looking at the teenager. "Fill it out, and then we'll talk."

The kid looked back at Lucas, obvious panic in his eyes.

"Javier!" It was Lilah, one of their cooks. "We have a situation back here."

"There's always a situation," Javier said to the three of them, rolling his eyes. "I'll be back. Get him started, Ronnie, would you?"

"On it," she said, fumbling through the shelf near the entrance where they kept that kind of paperwork.

"See," she heard Lucas say to Tyrone, "I told you to wear your best clothes."

Which meant the newer looking jeans Veronica had washed for him last night, as well as the one collared shirt in his back-pack. "Here's the application." She handed it to him along with a pen. "You can sit at that table over there and fill it out."

While the teenager worked laboriously at the table, chewing on his lip, Veronica stepped aside to talk to Lucas. "This is a surprise."

Lucas shrugged. "He doesn't want to go back to high school, not at this time of year. I think he can cyber school for the rest of the year. It's only about six weeks."

"His parents?" she asked.

"I called them." He sighed. "I confirmed that they're distant relatives of mine, not that I'm proud to admit it. Tyrone was right. They want nothing to do with him."

Veronica couldn't imagine. "The poor kid. That must be awful."

"It's wrong." Anger flashed in Lucas's face, so quickly that when it was gone Veronica wasn't sure she'd seen it. "Anyway, I told him he could rent a room from me—from Belo, actually—but he has to pay for it. Otherwise, he's got to go."

"Harsh!" She glared at him. "He's just a kid."

Lucas shrugged. "It doesn't do anyone any good to be a free-loader. Or to have nothing to do. Work is self-respect."

"And he decided to look for a job? And to stay at the house?"

"Belo okayed it. Are you comfortable having him there?"

"It's not any business of mine. I live in the cabin." She looked over at the young man, laboring over the job application. His shoulders hunched, he gripped the pencil tightly, slowly filling in the blanks like someone flunking a test in school. "I'm glad," she said softly. "I feel sorry for him."

"Me, too. But I may be taking on more than I can handle. He wants to get a drivers' license, too. I warned him that his staying here might be short term, but he's going to try."

She looked up at Lucas's worried face and something melted inside of her. Lucas was a good man. He would help out a distant family member he barely knew, even though a teen boy could be a real headache. But he hadn't even questioned it; he'd just done it. "That's good of you," she said.

"Are you willing to help me out, as long as you're here? Because..." He learned closer. "I honestly have no clue about how to take care of a teenage boy.""

"You were one, once." She laughed.

"It's been a long time since I was a teenager. Whereas you..."

"Yeah, yeah, I'm a baby compared to you." She looked at him, noticing the way his eyes crinkled at the corners when he laughed.

"Veronica!" Javier's voice was stern enough to break through whatever weird emotion Veronica was feeling. "Can you come here a minute?"

"Sure." She gave Lucas a last puzzled look and then walked over to the kitchen door.

The kitchen buzzed around her, the smell of onions sautéing, beans cooking, meat roasting. The waves and jokes of the cooks. The low sound of Mexican pop music.

It was all as familiar as her childhood. She loved El Corazon.

Yet she couldn't make it her life. Not anymore. She had to find her own way.

And while she saved money, she was going to practice doing just that. Finding her way. Making her own decisions. Taking risks.

She reached out and plucked a warm tortilla off the griddle.

"Want some butter and sugar with that?"

She grinned at Pedro, one of their longtime cooks. "You know me too well.". "Not this time."

"In here," Javier said, and led her to a quiet corner of the kitchen, ignoring Pedro's curious look. "Don't forget what I said before," Javier said.

She stared at him blankly. "About what?"

"About getting too close to Lucas. You don't need to be laughing and joking and flirting with him."

She took a step back and stared at him. "Are you serious? You asked me in here so you could big brother me again?"

"You seemed to need it." Javier glared.

"For the last time, I'm twenty-six." She started to turn away and then spun back. She wrapped her arms around her brother. "I appreciate you, Javier, I really do. But I can't let myself be sheltered by you forever." She narrowed her eyes at him. "It's time you and Molly have your own kids, so that you'll have someone who really needs taken care of." She felt okay saying it, because she knew from Molly that they wanted to start a family soon.

"Hey, that's not your business."

"No, it's not. See how great it feels when your family interferes in your life?" She smirked at him, even though she didn't like people who smirked. Then she strode across the kitchen and back out into the dining room, arriving just as Tyrone finished his application and stood. "Take this back to Mr. Quintana in the office," she said, leading the way to the kitchen door and pointing. "Right over there."

"Okay." The kid wasn't eager, but he did as she'd said.

Still annoyed over Javier and his bossiness, Veronica strode to where Lucas stood, arms crossed, looking attractive and a little dangerous. "Hey, I have an idea."

"Yeah? What's that?"

"I think we should take Lucas to church youth group," she said. "They have a movie night. I know because Trina goes."

"If he's comfortable with it, then sure. I'd like to see him get involved with some decent kids."

She hooked her arm through his. "And while he's there," she said, "I think you and I should go out."

5

S he hadn't really meant "go out." She couldn't have.

Lucas kept telling himself this as he drove Veronica from the church to the fire hall where some kind of benefit was being held.

"I'm not really dressed for anything formal," he said.

She looked down at her own simple dress. "Me, either. It's casual, though. Don't be uptight."'

She thought that of him, he knew. Thought that he was a worrier and no fun.

Maybe it was true.

But given his history, there was a part of him that deeply wanted to have fun. He wanted to live, really live, not just go through weeks and months in a robotic haze of work.

So he resolved to throw himself into this... he read the sign as they pulled into the parking night. "Karaoke night... benefits the foundation for..." He couldn't read the rest, but he was sure it was a good cause.

As soon as they got inside, people started calling Veronica's name.

"There she is!"

"Hey girl, sing with us!"

"Step aside, everyone, the Queen of Karaoke is here!"

"Are you?" he asked her as they found seats at an already crowded table.

She wrinkled her nose and grinned. "Kind of."

"Song choice?"

"I'll figure something out." She winked. "You okay if I leave you by yourself for a few?"

"Sure. I'll wander around." He mostly watched her, though. She walked down to the front where the DJ was and he could swear that every male in the room sat up and took notice.

She got in line, and he walked around, exploring and taking it in, trying not to let his reporter self make him nosey. Found a set of baskets up for raffle and bought a bunch of tickets. Then he got talking to the older woman behind the table about the benefit, what it was and whom it was for.

When he found out the benefit was for Corinna's Cupboard, the organization Evelyn Kujak had talked about, he started asking more questions. That led to a conversation about the need for lower-income people to have access to healthy foods.

Time flew by. It was a lot later when he felt a hand on his shoulder and jerked to attention. Veronica. "I missed hearing you sing!"

"You're working, aren't you?" She rolled her eyes. "And you," she said to the woman behind the table, "you're encouraging him. I'm trying to get this guy to stop being boring and have fun!"

"She's right," the woman said, and handed Lucas a business card. "Call me and we'll set something up to talk more. I'm interested in your project."

Veronica had Lucas by the hand and was tugging him across the room.

He found he didn't mind.

She stopped at the edge of a makeshift dance floor. "Come on. They're trying to get people to dance and no one will. We're going to set an example."

"We are?"

"We are."

Of their own accord, his arms curved to meet hers in classic tango stance. When he smelled her hair and felt her smooth skin, he couldn't have stopped himself if he'd tried.

After all he'd been through, he wanted to live. Not just exist, and not just work, but live. Life and health weren't to be taken for granted.

Someone on the stage must have seen how they were standing, because suddenly tango music started playing. He looked at Veronica. "You know how?"

She put up her thumb and finger two inches apart. "A little," she said. "Do you?"

He nodded. "Follow me."

She'd understated her skill; she was a great dancer. Soon, a small group of spectators stood in a semicircle and clapped, while other couples came out onto the dance floor to join in. He caught a hint of worry on her face and wondered what it was about, but he couldn't stop. They danced well together, close and coordinated, with good rhythm. More people flooded onto the dance floor.

The lights dimmed, and people crowded them, pushing them closer together as the music reverted to standard pop, stuff everyone could dance to. Obviously, the whole community supported this place. The smell of food mingled with the heat of the dancers' bodies.

He pulled Veronica closer and she froze. Their faces were inches apart.

He saw her slightly parted lips, the flush in her cheeks. Everything in him wanted to kiss her.

He leaned in.

She drew a deep breath, her brows pushing together.

He narrowed his eyes. "What did you think was going to happen," he asked, "when you asked me to dance?"

She stared at him. Then, suddenly, she twisted away. "I was wrong," she said.

"About what?" He was breathing hard.

"About you," she said. "You're not boring. You're dangerous."

The next morning, Lucas was still scolding himself when he heard a bang downstairs.

Belo couldn't be up yet, so it had to be Veronica.

"I could use some help down here!" The strident female voice—definitely *not* Veronica—thrust him straight back into childhood. He jogged down the steps double time.

And stopped dead when he saw Belo's housekeeper, Connie, struggling to get a wheelchair into the house, with a very large teenage boy wedged into it.

Hastily, he went to pull the front of the chair inside, frowning at the boy's unkempt state. Once they had the wheelchair in the middle of the kitchen, Lucas hugged the housekeeper who'd helped to raise him, then straightened his arms, keeping his hands on her shoulders. "What's going on?"

"She staged an intervention," the kid in the wheelchair said.

"My sister's health is so bad," Connie said, "that she's let Roscoe, here, get way out of shape."

"So Mom went to the rehab center, and I came here," Roscoe announced. "Surprise!"

Lucas frowned and rubbed his back, which had been hurting lately. "Does Belo know?" he asked Connie.

"Yes, of course. He said that you have taken in another young man, so perhaps these two will be good for one another."

"He's going to be psyched to meet me," Roscoe said, his tone sarcastic. "Not."

Apparently, their discussion had caught the attention of the people upstairs, because Veronica trotted down the stairs, closely followed by Tyrone. "We were playing Scrabble with Belo." She stopped when she saw Connie. "Oh, hello! I'm Veronica. I feel like we've met somewhere."

Connie's face creased into a million wrinkles, her version of a smile. "The market. You shop for El Corazon, and I shop for Mr. Picky, upstairs."

"Nice to see you again." She sat down on the edge of a chair, which put her at Roscoe's height, and held out a slim hand. "Hi. I'm Veronica."

Roscoe hesitated and then reached out and shook her hand. "Roscoe Valentine."

"He's my nephew," Connie explained, "and he's going to be staying here while my sister gets some health issues resolved."

Lucas felt like he was reeling. When he'd decided to move back to Arcadia Valley, he'd expected to come home to an empty, lonely house. But the place was rapidly filling up. He turned, beckoned Tyrone forward, and introduced him.

Connie greeted him warmly, but Roscoe just grunted and Tyrone did the same. In addition to being a couple of years younger, Roscoe's weight and apparent disability added difference.

"Do you have a room in mind for Roscoe?" Lucas asked Connie. "I'm assuming first floor would be best."

"I don't have to be in a wheelchair." Roscoe leaned forward and pushed and rocked himself out of the chair and into a standing position.

"Well my lands, son, why'd you let me go through all that to push you through the door?" Connie asked, her voice indignant.

"I was tired," Roscoe said, a whine sneaking into his voice.

Tyrone snorted, just a little, but it was enough to make Roscoe glare. "You have a comment, pip-squeak?"

Lucas stepped between the two boys. "Look. You're both welcome here, but there are house rules. One is civility. Another is..." He hesitated, glanced at Veronica.

"Chores," she said. "Everyone has to do chores."

Roscoe's eye roll was monumental, Tyrone's more subtle.

"Roscoe and Connie, you must have some unpacking to do," Lucas said. "So Tyrone and I will make lunch."

"But I don't know how to—"

"Time to learn," Veronica said, giving Lucas a wink that left him breathless. "I wonder if Belo would like to come down for lunch?"

"Does he ever?" Lucas asked Connie.

She looked doubtful. "It's rare, but he's able to, I think."

"Then let's get him down here to meet our new... guests," Veronica suggested. "Connie, I'm mostly working as an assistant to Lucas, but I've been helping out around the house while you were gone, and helping with Belo. We'll have to talk about whether that arrangement should continue."

Connie's face froze. "I can handle the house."

"Connie," Lucas said, soothing her. "It looks like you have just a little bit else on your hands."

"Namely me," Roscoe said, smiling in a way that clearly showed his kinship to Connie. "Aunt Connie thinks she can get me out here on the farm and get me to slim down, so I can go to school without being bullied."

"You could cyber school," Lucas suggested, "like Tyrone is going to do. In fact, what grade are you in?"

"Roscoe's a smart boy," Connie said. "He's in eleventh grade, even though he's only fifteen."

"Tyrone, too. Maybe you boys could study together."

More mutual eye rolls. "Let's meet up and discuss it over lunch in half an hour," Lucas suggested.

WHEN THEY ALL sat down to lunch a short while later, Veronica couldn't help wondering how they'd get through it.

The two teen boys seemed to have independently come to the decision to be silent. Belo, meanwhile, was firing questions at them while complaining about the food Connie had prepared.

"We're eating healthy," Connie said severely. "After lunch, Roscoe and I will go to the market and pick up some more fresh things."

Roscoe let out a windy sigh.

"Arcadia Valley is a great place to come for your health," Veronica said, trying to interject happy enthusiasm into the conversation. "There are all kinds of restaurants that are farm to table, including El Corazon. Where Tyrone is working, I think? Did you get the job?"

The boy nodded, not looking up from his plate.

Lucas opened his mouth, obviously about to demand respect. She shook her head at him. "There are several organic farms and the farmer's market. Lots of people interested in sustainable living."

Belo waved a dismissive hand. "It's nothing new," he said. "It's how we used to live on the land, eating what we farmed and making our own way. It just has a different name."

Lucas reached over to put an arm around his grandfather. "You just helped me put the finishing touch on my new book idea."

"Ooh, tell us about it." Veronica was excited to have the topic further pinned down. Up until now, they'd just been poking around, as Lucas put it. Too ambiguous.

"Old and new sustainability," Lucas said. "The similarities between today's organic, whole-food ideas and the way our ancestors lived on the land."

"So, a little history, and a little food stuff?" she asked.

"Sounds boring," Tyrone said.

"Yup." Roscoe reached across the table and forked more salad out of the bowl.

"No. Uh-uh," Veronica said, automatically channeling her own mother. "You use the serving utensils, not your fork. And if a dish is across the table, you ask for it to be passed to you."

"With a 'please' and a 'thank you,'" Connie added with an approving nod at Veronica.

"It's not like we're at a restaurant," Tyrone protested.

At least the two boys were on the same page, finally. "The manners you use at home become automatic," Lucas said. "You'll be able to go anywhere and feel confident if you learn the right way to do things at home."

Roscoe sighed heavily. "May I *please* have the bread?"

"Of course." Veronica passed the basket to him.

"You shouldn't eat so much," Tyrone said. "You're fat."

Roscoe flinched, almost indiscernibly. "Well, you're a..."

Whatever Roscoe had planned to say in response was halted by Connie's fingertip on his mouth.

Meanwhile, Lucas had gripped Tyrone's shoulder. "Inappropriate. Apologize."

"Sorry," Tyrone muttered.

The three adults glanced at each other. They had to band together and help these boys.

Roscoe *was* heavy, and his color wasn't good. He didn't look healthy, and his poor grooming had to be a negative for his social life with other teens. At least he had some family who cared about him, though. Tyrone appeared to be entirely on his own.

Veronica sent up a quick prayer of thanks for her big, extended, noisy family. Yes, her brothers smothered her, but it was acres better than being left alone.

For the first time, she questioned her plan of leaving Arcadia Valley and settling somewhere else. Who would pick her up if she fell down?

"Tyrone, maybe you can help Roscoe and Connie carry in the rest of their things," Lucas said. "And then don't you start work at four?"

Roscoe glanced up, the first indication of interest he'd shown.

"Would *you* like to look for a job?" Veronica asked.

Roscoe glanced over at Connie.

She shrugged. "No reason not to, as long as your employer knows it may be temporary."

"You could try El Corazon," Veronica said. "A couple of their people quit recently. Tyrone got one of the openings, but I'm pretty sure they're still looking for help."

"He's too—"

"Enough." Lucas's stern voice and glare stopped whatever Tyrone had been about to say. "Let's help with the dishes and then with the unloading."

"I'll get the dishes," Veronica said quickly. She almost needed a break.

But as the boys started carrying things in under Connie's direction, Lucas followed her into the kitchen. When she turned from putting down an armload of dishes, he was right behind her. He opened his mouth to say something, but then he went still, his gaze dropping to her lips.

She drew in a sharp breath and backed up until the edge of the sink blocked her from going any farther.

He stepped back, looked away almost as if he were collecting himself, and then turned back to face her. "We've got ourselves a situation here," he said. "All of a sudden, two teenage boys. I wouldn't blame you if you wanted to reconsider our agreement."

He was giving her an out. And in light of the odd feelings she was having whenever she was near him, she really ought to take him up on it. Because falling for him meant she'd never get away from Arcadia Valley.

But how could she leave him to handle this *situation,* as he'd called it, alone?

"Are you kidding?" she asked against her own better judgment. "You need more help than ever, now."

WHAT WAS HE DOING? Lucas wondered later that afternoon as he finished his last deadlift at the Arcadia Valley YMCA and groaned. A little bit from the relief, and a lot because of the state of affairs at home.

He'd come back to Arcadia Valley to take care of Belo and regroup, try to figure out what his life was going to be in light of the past few years' events. He'd expected that he might run into a few old friends, since he'd partly grown up here. But he'd figured it would be a quiet life, maybe a little lonely, as he figured out the next book project and helped Belo heal.

Instead, it looked like he was going to get more deeply involved with Tyrone and Roscoe. Two teen boys who needed guidance and mentoring.

Lucas wasn't good at that sort of thing, or didn't think so. The truth was, he'd never really mentored anyone before.

He'd lived a selfish life.

But that was all changing. He'd had a wake-up call, and it had reminded him that a life of working and constant travel wasn't all it was cracked up to be.

He grabbed some free weights and started his bicep curls. Funny, he was almost more religious about working out than about church, but that needed to change, too. Starting with taking Belo to mass this Saturday night or Sunday, and he'd do that as long and as often as the old man wanted him to, making up for lost time both with his grandfather and with God. But there was more to it than churchgoing. He'd been reading scripture, slowly and carefully, thinking it through. He knew all too well that it was possible to go to church and space out, let the incense and the music and the words flow over you in a vague, feel-good sort of way. Or a feel-bored sort of way, as when he was a teenager.

He wanted more.

"Lucas!" It was Daniel Quintana, just sitting up from bench pressing a cool 200 pounds. "How's it feel to be back home?"

"Good," he said, surprised to realize that it was true. Despite the complications and the questions, he felt more centered and right in Arcadia Valley than he'd felt in the past few years. "It's a good place, and getting better."

"For me, too." Daniel stood, gestured at the bench and weights, and quirked an eyebrow. "Want me to spot you?"

"Sure." He added 20 more to Daniel's 200 and got into position. He didn't know Daniel well, but he liked what he knew. Daniel was the thoughtful type, less domineering than Javier, more serious than Alex. A reader and a thinker.

Daniel helped him through a couple of reps and then, as Lucas strained with a third, Daniel spoke up. "You keeping it respectful with my sister?"

Lucas opened his eyes to find that Daniel's hands were open below the bar, ready to catch the weights but not holding them. There was no mistaking the threat in his eyes.

"Yeah," Lucas grunted out, and was rewarded by Daniel's assisting him in putting down the weight.

Point taken.

After they'd both done shoulder work, they walked over

toward the locker room together. In the doorway, Daniel stopped him. "How's your health?" he asked.

Lucas narrowed his eyes at Daniel. "I'm good. Why?"

Daniel lifted his chin. "Not my business, but... if you ever need anything here in the Valley, I can give you some references. Or a listening ear."

Right. Daniel was a chiropractor. Lucas blew out a sigh. "So it shows, huh?"

Daniel nodded slowly. "Yeah. If you know what to look for." He clapped Lucas on the shoulder. "Stay strong, brother." And he strode out of the gym.

Lucas looked after him thoughtfully. The man had gone through a lot; Veronica had mentioned his recent marriage, and Connie had filled him in on some of the heartache that had led up to it. Daniel's daughter had undergone a kidney transplant and was doing well, but there had been a distance to go, emotionally, before that could be the case.

Yet Daniel, quiet Daniel, had persevered and found love.

Was love in the cards for Lucas, too?

No. It couldn't be, not marriage and children and all the things Daniel had. Not with all Lucas's issues. He had to content himself with caring for Belo. And apparently, for a couple of at-loose-ends teen boys. It would have to be enough.

His grandfather's wish for him to get married and sire a son, notwithstanding.

The soulful eyes of his very pretty assistant notwithstanding.

He wanted love and connection and intimacy, too. He wanted it all. But nobody got it all.

6

F ive days later, Veronica sank down at the big house's kitchen table and put her head in her hands.

The teenagers were off to work at El Corazon—though due back any minute—Connie and Lucas were both out, and Belo was asleep. She had the downstairs all to herself.

It felt like the first time she'd stopped moving since she'd come to live here. And even though she was exhausted, her thoughts swarmed around a whole set of topics—her own future, her work here, and especially Lucas.

As tension tightened her stomach, the wise words of Mama Beatriz came to mind. *When your mind races, you need to race to God.*

She let her forehead drop to her hands and closed her eyes. *Father, I'm confused, I'm restless, and I don't know what to do.*

Of course, God knew all that. But it seemed to help to put it into words.

Her idea of playacting a relationship with Lucas, of practicing on him, now struck her as the height of stupidity. How ridiculous, to think she could learn about something as important as relationships while playing a childish game.

How wrong, to use another human being in that way.

And her comeuppance had already arrived:. Her heart was getting more and more drawn to Lucas, and yet she didn't mean to stay around Arcadia Valley. And she didn't want to be with a man who reminded her so much of her domineering brothers.

And yet she was needed here; it wasn't as if she could just leave. She'd agreed to take the job as Lucas's assistant. And now, with the boys staying here, and Belo, Lucas truly couldn't do it alone.

Thank heavens for Connie, who kept her nephew in line and excelled at cooking, whether it meant preparing something delicate to tempt Belo's appetite, or hearty to appeal to the boys.

She really was blessed to have this time and space to think about where to go next. Compared to a lot of people who worked dangerous, physical jobs or raised multiple kids, she had it easy. She just needed to keep her heart and her emotions in line.

"Hey, Veronica!" There was a pounding at her door.

She opened it to discover the two boys, Tyrone and Roscoe, out of breath. "What's going on? Is Belo okay?" She knew Lucas was out, doing some kind of research he hadn't wanted her to help with. In fact, he'd acted a little mysterious about where he was going and what he was doing, and she'd felt a flash of jealousy that he might be taking someone out on a date.

But that wasn't her business. She was Lucas's assistant, nothing more, and if he wanted to give her an afternoon off, that was all to the good. She could use the time to catch up on paperwork and look for a job and place to live for the autumn.

"I don't know anything about Belo, I haven't seen him," Roscoe said, his voice tight with tension, "but Aunt Connie isn't doing so well. My mom needs her again, and she's out back, crying her eyes out."

Veronica stuck her feet into flip flops and ran across the yard with the boys. She found Connie leaning on the car and clutching her cell phone, concern and worry in her eyes.

"What happened?" Veronica put an arm around the older woman.

"It's my sister. She got some bad test results, and she needs someone to drive her back and forth to the hospital. But I can't leave again just after I returned. I have a job here. I have to keep up the house for the men, do the cooking and housework. And you, Roscoe..." She looked over at her nephew, frowning.

"I'll go home with you. I can help Mom. I've done it before." But Roscoe didn't sound convinced, and Veronica thought she knew why. He'd been gaining self-esteem, just in his few days of working at El Corazon. And he'd been doing great in cyber high school. In just a week, he'd come a long way from the boy who'd entered the house in a wheelchair. His life had taken an upswing since he'd come to Arcadia Valley, concern about his mother notwithstanding.

"That will just upset her." Connie bit her lip and held onto Roscoe's arm. "She's so glad you're set up in school and working a job."

"He's got to stay here with us," Veronica heard herself say. "Don't you worry about it. I'm supposed to be Lucas's assistant and do other duties as required. I'll watch over Roscoe. And I'll do the housework, with the boys' help. Right?"

They looked at each other. "Sure," Roscoe said, and Tyrone mumbled his assent.

"But what about the cooking?" Connie fretted.

"That's the only thing," Veronica admitted. "I'm a terrible cook."

"I can show you what to do, leave you instructions...."

Veronica let out a half-laugh. "You can, but... I'm the child of restaurant owners and I still burn water."

"I cannot leave, then."

"We'll figure something out. You go get your things together, and don't give the work here a second thought."

She'd manage, somehow. What choice did she have?

Connie hugged her. "If you're sure... thank you. Thank you!"

"WE DID IT," Roscoe growled the next day as he flung open the back door. It banged against the kitchen wall, and Veronica winced.

Behind him, Tyrone snapped "give me a hand with this!"

"Boys—"

Roscoe turned, tried to push the screen door open wider, and ended up tripping Tyrone. The boy pitched forward into the kitchen, the large box of vegetables he'd brought home spilling out onto the floor.

"Now look what you did," Roscoe said.

"It wasn't my fault," Tyrone snarled, kicking at a stray onion as it rolled into his path.

"Boys!" Veronica was so not equipped for this. "Pick those up, both of you, and stack them by the sink in categories."

Roscoe knelt to do so, the effort making him breathe hard.

"Whaddya mean, categories?" Tyrone asked.

"She means put greens with greens, and fruit with fruit, dummy." Roscoe glanced over at Veronica. "Right?"

"It's never right to call someone dummy," she said sternly. When Tyrone smirked, she added, "or any other name. Understood?"

"Yeah," they both said with a notable lack of conviction.

"And that *is* what I meant about categories. I'm going to start with onions, so pick all of those up first. Once everything's off the floor, I want one of you to sweep it, since there's dirt all over now. The other can chop."

"I'll sweep," Tyrone said quickly. "I ain't touching onions."

Honestly, Veronica felt the same way. She knew she was going to botch this. A cook she wasn't.

Maybe she should call Javier, at least get his suggestions on what to do with all this food. Lucas had asked for more vegetables, and it had seemed like a good idea to send the boys out to the farmer's market for them. She just hadn't pictured them showing up with such a large box, and such a mishmash.

But calling Javier, or even Alex, would negate what she was trying to do. She'd never prove her independence from her brothers.

And for whatever reason, she wanted to prove to Lucas that she could make it domestically.

Not that he'd be impressed or interested. But if she was ever going to have a relationship, not with Lucas of course, but with anyone, then she needed to show she could run a household, and that included cooking.

Roscoe was bending to pick up the last of the vegetables when Tyrone whispered an insult, something about Roscoe's weight.

Roscoe turned and gave Tyrone a swift punch in the arm. A weak hit that didn't look like it hurt, but still wasn't to be tolerated.

"Chop. Now." She pointed to the onions and pulled out a large cutting board.

Too late, she wondered about the wisdom of giving an angry young boy a knife.

Tyrone got out the broom and did what looked like a purposefully ineffectual job of sweeping. Once she got the oil heated up, she started dumping in Roscoe's neat onion squares.

Were they supposed to sizzle that loud?

She went over to the cupboard that held Connie's few, dusty cookbooks; the older woman had normally just cooked from her own knowledge, but before she'd left, she'd revealed to Veronica her stash. She pulled out a couple and started paging through.

"What are we even making here?" Roscoe asked her a few minutes later.

"Ummmmm, soup. We're making soup, and we're going to freeze containers of it for later, so we'll make a lot." Vegetable soup would probably be the best way to use up all of that food quickly. And if they had homemade vegetable soup, she wouldn't feel so bad about serving hot dogs or grilled cheese as an accompaniment.

She walked over to inspect the onions. The sizzling was louder now, and a pungent smell reached her nose at the same moment that Tyrone came to look over her shoulder. "They're burning."

"Brilliant, Einstein," Roscoe said, shoving another pile of onions toward Veronica.

"If you knew they were burning, why didn't you say so?" Veronica turned off the heat, leaned back against the wall, and slowly sank to the floor.

This was beyond her. She thought of her mother, raising four kids, running El Corazon with Dad, and finding time to cook delicious meals every night.

By comparison, Veronica was a failure.

She glanced over and noticed something on the floor. A keychain she'd seen Roscoe holding as if it were made of gold.

Lucas and Connie had somehow arranged for Roscoe to have the use of a car. Tyrone was riding along, for now, but saving his money to buy a car, too.

She picked up the keychain and saw a photo of Roscoe and his mother, arms around each other. The back of the keychain frame said "Love You To The Moon and Back."

Her throat tightened as she looked up at the two boys.

Roscoe was scraping at the burned onions while Tyrone stood at the sink, clumsily rinsing greens.

Roscoe was just a child, scared about his mom's health, missing her. Now, even his aunt wasn't around.

As for Tyrone, his family didn't even want him.

And here she was worrying about whether she could cook like her own mother, when she knew the answer perfectly well: she couldn't.

But that wasn't the most important part of mothering.

She stood up, walked over to stand in between the two tall boys, and put an arm around each. "Thanks for helping," she said.

Roscoe leaned in a little, but Tyrone twisted away.

"Hey, what's going on here?"

It was Lucas. She let go of the boys and turned to see him standing in the doorway.

"She done stunk up your kitchen," Tyrone said.

Roscoe snorted out a laugh, then quickly suppressed it.

Veronica sighed. "It's true. I'm a terrible cook," she admitted. "But I do have a secret weapon. And it looks like it's time to bring it—her—out."

7

The next week, Lucas pushed back his chair and looked around the table. "That was a good meal," he said, trying to keep the surprise out of his voice.

"*Muy bueno*," Belo said. He'd suddenly started coming down to dinner, and Lucas had to suspect it was because of all the liveliness in the house now.

Well, that, or the presence of Veronica's grandmother, who'd come to stay with Veronica in the cottage to give her a hand with the cooking. It turned out *she* was the secret weapon Veronica had come up with.

Veronica's grandmother's eyes twinkled. "This child is learning. She may make some man a good wife, yet."

"Abuela!" Veronica's cheeks grew pink. "Cooking isn't necessarily related to marriage."

"And men can cook," Lucas felt obligated to explain.

Nonetheless, he was starting to feel like he was part of a family, the sort-of father of it. The two teen boys followed him around a lot, so he'd been teaching them about research as well as some home repairs and street skills.

Meanwhile, Veronica was sharing housekeeping duties with him. And she and her grandmother were rocking it out in the cooking department. They'd actually taken every member of the household aside and asked about their food likes and dislikes.

He'd fine-tuned his request for more fruits and vegetables by asking specifically for fresh greens, cabbage, and broccoli, ideas he'd been getting in his book research. The diet that would help him, health wise, would also help Roscoe lose some weight and Tyrone to calm down.

The boys were also learning a lot about chores, but enough was enough. "If you'll help Belo and Abuela take their things into the living room and get the fire going, you guys can go do your gaming." He'd broken down and bought a gaming console and the boys loved it. Meanwhile, Belo and Abuela were starting to have an evening routine of talking in the living room by the fire, stoking it up a little too warm for the younger set, but perfect for elders.

That left him and Veronica to do the cleanup. But she'd done enough. "You go ahead and take it easy or go out," he said to her as they carried dishes into the kitchen.

"No, that's okay." She rinsed a plate.

He put his hands on her shoulders and turned her around. "I mean it," he said. "It's Saturday night. Why don't you go out dancing with your friends?"

She shook her head, wiggled away from him, and turned back to the dishes. "I don't really go out that much."

"Why not? Your brothers made it sound like you're out all the time and carefree."

"My brothers don't know everything."

He started putting leftover food into containers. "Sounds like there's a story there."

"Maybe." She glanced at him. "Look, Lucas, aren't there

some things you'd rather keep private? Things about yourself, things that have happened, that you just don't want anyone else bothering you about?"

Lucas studied her and nodded. "Yes. Yes, I do have something like that."

Curiosity flared in her eyes. "Want to tell me?"

"No, I do not," he said. "Not unless you tell me yours."

"Maybe someday," she hedged. "Why do you keep your *thing* a secret?"

"Because I want to handle it myself," he said. "Because I don't want everyone to look at me with pity."

She nodded once. "That's exactly why I don't tell anyone mine."

"If I promise not to look at you with pity, or to interfere, will you tell me?" he asked.

"Why? Why do you want to know?"

That was the million dollar question. Why *did* he want to know?

Why did being here, in this kitchen, with this woman, bring on such a crazy mix of feelings?

He stared out the window. The sinking sun cast a golden glow. White trillium and forsythia grew wild near the house, punctuated by drooping pink heads of Prairie Smoke. The soft green fields stretched off into the horizon, hopeful young soybean plants poking their way into a springtime world, trying to gain strength before the dry hot weather hit.

Beyond the fields, off to the left, high bluffs pushed against the bright blue sky. Everything he saw was as it had been in his childhood, and the permanence of the land reminded him that God had a bigger plan and a longer timeline than mere humans could discern.

He wondered what Veronica's secret was. Some hurt in love,

some disappointment with work or family? "All I can do is listen," he told her. "I certainly don't have any answers, but sometimes it can help to share what you're going through."

She ran hot water into the sink and started putting in the water glasses, part of his grandmother's collection and too fragile for the dishwasher. "You won't tell my brothers?"

"Of course not."

She studied his face, then nodded. "When I was in Twin Falls," she said, "Something... something happened to me."

"What kind of a something?" He took a sponge and started wiping down the counter so he wouldn't be staring directly at her. Sometimes, a little space helped a person get a story out. He'd learned that in his years of interviewing sources.

"It was... a man at work." She wasn't looking at him, just methodically scrubbing and rinsing glasses. "He was my boss and he..." She trailed off, letting the water run over one of the glasses.

Heat rose in Lucas's neck and his hand clenched on the sponge. He took a deep breath and let it out slowly. "What did he do?"

She sighed, shook her head. "He kept asking me to come into his office after hours," she said. "He'd stand too close, or he'd ask if I could get a stain off his shirt, things to make me touch him."

Anger boiled hot inside Lucas. "Did you report him?"

She lifted her hands, palms up. "I tried to, but since he was the editor in chief, there really wasn't much chain of command above him." She rolled her eyes. "I asked in personnel, and the woman who worked there just laughed and told me to try to stay out of his office. That he did it to all the girls, and that it was no big deal."

"Whoa," he said. "Do they know what year this is? What's been in the news? The world has changed from those days, thank heavens. What happened next?"

"One night, I was working on a story, all involved in it, and I realized everyone else except my boss had left. I hurried to finish, and grabbed my coat and purse, and then he came out of his office." She swallowed hard. "He ordered me to come into his, and when I wouldn't, he pushed me against the desk and..." She turned away.

He wanted to wrap an arm around her, to comfort her. But of course, that wasn't the right thing to do, not now. Instead, he took her hand and led her to the kitchen table, and pulled out a chair for her.

She sat down, staring at the table.

"Do you want to tell me more?" Lucas spun a chair around and straddled it, facing her. He was out of his element here, not least because he cared so much for Veronica. He couldn't be objective or wise, because his heart was involved.

His heart was involved. He put that thought aside to examine later.

"He didn't... finish the assault," she said, "because the cleaning staff came in. I was never so glad to see anyone in my life! He let me up, and I ran out of there."

There was a world of detail that she wasn't including, like how far things had gone. But that was her business. Any type of harassment or assault was traumatic to the victim. "Did you report it to the police?"

She shook her head. "No. I just gave notice at work, and broke the lease on my apartment, and came running back to Arcadia Valley." She looked up at him, her mouth twisted, tears standing in her eyes. "I know I should have reported him to the authorities, should have been strong. But I didn't have it in me, Lucas. I wasn't brave enough to be the one who reported him."

"That's understandable." He consciously loosened his clenched fists. Getting angry wouldn't help, not right now. He pushed off the chair and stood, shaking his head, pacing restlessly. "What a sorry excuse for a man."

"I know. And I can't let him define me, Lucas. I came running back here, and I'm trying to regather my strength, but I need to get back out there, you know? I can't hide in Arcadia Valley, hide behind my brothers, work in my family's business forever. Not if I want to live the life God's called me to."

He felt like pulling her into his arms, but she was talking about independent strength, not resting in a man's protection. "What do you feel like God's called you to do?"

"To be a journalist, using the media and technology to tell the hard stuff, expose the truth." She held up a hand. "I know, I know. The irony is that I can't tell my own truth. Maybe someday, I will."

"But for now..."

"For now, I want to save up my money and build up my resume—because *he* won't give me any kind of recommendation —and then move away from Arcadia Valley again."

"Move where?" He didn't want her to go. But the last thing she needed was for him to tell her what to do.

She shrugged. "Maybe a big city, DC or LA. Maybe overseas. I pray about it every day, but so far, I haven't discerned my next step."

"You will." He had to admire her. What she wanted to do was much like he'd wanted, years ago. The trouble was, he'd gotten his wandering over with, and now he wanted to put down roots.

Unfortunately, he was starting to care for Veronica a lot. To think, however wrongly, of including her in his future plans.

But that wasn't what she needed, or wanted. For Veronica, the future wasn't about roots, but wings.

"Thanks for listening," she said. Now it was she who took his hand, tugging him back toward the sink. Her whole face and bearing seemed lighter. That was the power of confession.

When they reached the sink she dropped his hand and turned to face him. She was standing close, almost as tall as he was. He could feel her breath.

"So what's *your* secret, Lucas?" she asked.

8

Veronica looked up at Lucas, standing so close, the golden light from the window illuminating his face.

It was a good face. A good face to match a good soul. He'd listened to her story, a story she'd told no one else, and he hadn't turned away nor, even worse, blamed her for what had happened. Instead, he'd instantly sided with her.

That was food for thought. If she'd reported the assault, maybe other people would have reacted like Lucas.

It was something to consider another day. Someday soon.

Today, she felt lighter, almost playful with the relief of sharing her burden. "Well?" she asked, daring to reach out a hand and touch his chest. "What's your big secret?"

"I..." He looked down at her hand, smiled a little, then shook his head and chuffed out a breath and stepped back. "I'll tell you sometime, but not tonight."

"Promise?" She didn't know what was putting the breathlessness in her voice. This was Lucas, her brothers' friend, her employer. Lucas, who was ten years older than she was.

Right now, though, he just seemed like a man, and Veronica was feeling things she'd never felt before. Propelled by that unfamiliar force, she took a step toward him. "Thanks for listening," she murmured, close to his face. "I'll return the favor soon."

Their lips were inches apart. He put his hands on her shoulders, lightly, and stepped away.

But he didn't let go.

She didn't want him to. She wanted to be closer. She stepped toward him again.

"Veronica—"

He was going to tell her to go away, because she was like a little sister to him. She knew he was going to do that, and she didn't want him to, so she rose to her tiptoes and brushed her lips against his.

The impact of that small, quick connection was so powerful that she didn't understand, at first, the loud, angry voice she heard.

The banging of a door. Lucas putting her firmly away and stepping in front of her.

Then she looked over his shoulder and saw the problem.

Javier.

"What on earth?" Her brother stormed toward them like some ancient warrior, his dark eyebrows drawn together, and anger pursing his lips. He grabbed Lucas's shoulder and tried to shove him away.

Lucas stood firm between her and her brother, his hand out, knocking away Javier's arm, his hand blocking Javier's chest. "Slow down," he ordered. "You're in my home."

"That's *my* sister," Javier snarled.

Veronica waited for Lucas to tell her brother that she was the one who'd started it, that he'd tried to push her away.

He didn't do it. "I understand that, and we can talk. But you need to back off."

"*You* need to back off." But Javier did take a step back. "You okay, Ronnie?"

The pet name made her mouth curve up in a smile, brought back all the times Javier, or Alex or Daniel, had warned off bullies on the playground or interested men at church or a community dance. No wonder she was single at twenty-six! "I'm fine. It was my—"

Lucas interrupted her, still blocking her from Javier with his bulky frame. "She's fine, and what you saw won't happen again."

It *wouldn't*?

"You better believe it won't," Javier said.

This was ridiculous. She stepped out from behind Lucas. Yeah, she was glad he'd intervened, because Javier still scared her some when he was angry. But that was something she needed to get over.

And yeah, this moment called to mind the exact process she'd gone through as a kid: from being scared of her angry older brother to yelling "you're not the boss of me!"

She tried to age up the concept. "Javier, I'm perfectly able to stand up for myself."

"Not from the looks of things. I want you to promise me—"

"*I'll* promise you," Lucas said. "In addition to the fact that that was inappropriate, I have my own good reasons for staying unencumbered."

Unencumbered? She was an encumbrance?

Halting footsteps sounded outside the kitchen door. "*Mi nieto*, you *must* become encumbered. And this young woman is a fine prospect." Belo stomped as best he could into the kitchen, his cane punctuating every step.

Veronica sank down into a kitchen chair and rested her face in her hands. No way could she withstand *three* men who thought they were the essence of *machismo* and who were attempting to govern her fate.

Her grandmother had no such qualms. She marched right into the middle of Belo, Javier, and Lucas. "You men! Leave this poor young woman alone to make her choices. She is not a string of chile peppers on sale at the market!"

All three men froze for a moment—out of respect for Abuela, or out of recognition that her words were true, it wasn't clear—and then they fell all over themselves with assurances and apologies. They weren't looking at Veronica that way. They were looking out for her. She was a fine young woman, cut out for motherhood.

"It's true that she should marry, but not your grandson, Señor," Javier said to Belo. "He's too old for her."

Belo snorted.

Veronica's head whipped around to see Lucas's reaction to that point. He didn't *seem* old. He was handsome and muscular and successful.

It was a very appealing package, and his age didn't enter into the mix.

"You're right," Lucas said unexpectedly. He was rubbing the back of his neck like it hurt. "Veronica is a lovely woman, and I have no doubt that she'll marry and form a family. But I'm not the person with whom that should happen."

Veronica's face heated and tears pushed against the backs of her eyes. Had she imagined the attraction between them? Had she forced that kiss on him?

Apparently so.

He wasn't interested in her. Which hurt, because she suddenly realized she was growing more and more interested in him.

She wanted to explore a relationship with Lucas. Oh, it had started as a playful thing, practicing her relationship skills and independence on a safe person.

And it turned out he *was* certainly safe, because he had absolutely no interest in her.

But unfortunately, somewhere along the line, she'd fallen for him. Fallen off a cliff, fallen into the clover, fallen somewhere close to love.

Which was a very, very bad thing for all of her dreams and goals.

Luckily, those weren't at risk. He'd deemed their kiss as "inappropriate." Declared it wouldn't happen again.

Humiliation and hurt—and loss—jerked her to her feet, and the chair tipped over behind her with a loud crash. "You all just go ahead and discuss my characteristics and future," she said into the sudden silence. "I'm going... out."

She slammed out the door and stomped toward the cabin, but the truth was, she didn't feel like going out. She felt like staying in and curling up in a tiny ball and crying her eyes out.

9

The next day, Lucas held open the door of the Baxter Family Bakery for his grandfather. After a sullen early-morning appointment with Belo's heart doctor, Lucas hoped that some locally-famous sweets would make him feel better.

Lucas needed to get Belo off the "get married" bandwagon. It was downright embarrassing, now that he was openly telling everyone about his aspirations for Lucas. Belo had trumpeted the importance of Lucas settling down to the doctor this morning, which was bad.

But yesterday's outburst, when Belo had told Javier and Veronica Quintana about it, was even worse.

Veronica. Lucas helped Belo to a seat and then went to stand in line, his mind gnawing on what had happened yesterday.

He hadn't had any intention of kissing her. Not before, and certainly not after she'd revealed her Twin Falls experience with her boss.

In fact, as soon as she'd described the workplace environment, he'd determined to talk to her about whether she'd feel comfortable pressing charges or filing a harassment lawsuit.

But kissing her? Since he couldn't marry her, he had no business getting close enough to kiss her.

Not only that, but kissing her put him in the same camp as the slimy boss, since he was her employer.

True, it wasn't he who'd initiated that kiss. It had been her doing, and that was tormenting him.

Why had she done it? Gratitude for his willingness to listen? Relief to get her unhappy story off her chest?

Real caring and attraction?

"Lucas." It was Malachi Baxter, who usually wasn't behind the counter. "Earth to Lucas. Do you want to order?"

"Sure, man, how're you doing?" He'd heard that Malachi had recently married, something he wouldn't have expected from the guy's reputation as a reclusive genius.

But sure enough, Malachi looked happier than Lucas had ever seen him.

"I'll take a bran muffin for my grandfather and a lemon poppy seed for me," he said. "And a sack of... what's most popular with teenaged boys?"

"Gotta be the king-sized chocolate chip cookies," Malachi said. "I'll get you started. Coffee, too? Are you eating here?"

Lucas glanced over at Belo, who was staring absently out the window. The old man was tired, which meant they probably shouldn't stay long. But on the other hand, he didn't get out enough, and the sunshine and socializing might do him good. "Sure, two coffees and we'll eat here, with the bag of cookies to go."

Within minutes, he and his grandfather were biting into their giant muffins... and even though Belo had insisted on trading, saying he wasn't going to eat "old man bran," Lucas's taste buds practically exploded with the honey-rich heartiness. Knowing the whole grains and nuts were good medicine helped him feel okay about scarfing down the whole thing in less than a minute. Then he watched Belo savor his muffin more slowly as the bakery hummed behind them, voices from the kitchen blending with friendly greetings from customers.

Belo put down the second half of the muffin and wiped powdered sugar off his mouth. "All of the Baxter brothers, except one, are married," he said pointedly. "I heard *his* wife is expecting." He nodded toward Malachi.

"That's great." And it was, but Lucas knew where his grandfather was headed. "Belo, we need to talk."

"*Sí,*" the old man said. "You need to stop delaying and court Veronica Quintana."

Like many older people with hearing problems, Belo spoke loudly, and Lucas winced and looked around.

There were no other customers seated, and the two women in line were talking to each other with animation, clearly not listening to anything else going on around them. Lucas looked at Malachai, ready to be embarrassed if the guy had heard, and then remembered that he was deaf.

He turned back to his grandfather. "Belo, I don't want to court Veronica."

"Don't lie to me." Belo leaned forward and poked a finger at Lucas. "I've seen the way you look at her."

"Well. Okay." Lucas spread his hands. "Of course I like her. She's beautiful and smart and kind. Who wouldn't like her?"

"A good woman," Belo said. "Just the woman for you."

Lucas blew out a breath. Belo had a one-track mind in regard to what he wanted. "She's *not* the woman for me. I'm not the man for her."

"You are my last hope, the last of the Ruiz line!" Belo's fingers pinched together as he gestured with his hands. "You must allow love into your life, *mi nieto*! Not only for me, for our line, but for yourself!"

"I understand that, Belo, but—"

"No but! You must be a coward no longer!"

"I have cancer!"

The bakery suddenly seemed too quiet. Belo's mouth, open for more argument, hung open.

Lucas squeezed his eyes shut for an instant. He hadn't intended to tell Belo this way, hadn't intended to tell him, period. He leaned forward and took Belo's hand. "Look, I'm sorry. I shouldn't have told you."

Belo stared at their linked hands and then looked into Lucas's face. "How bad?"

"I'm done with my treatments and the doctors are optimistic. But I don't feel like I'm in any position to even date a woman, let alone marry her."

Belo nodded, frowning.

"I go to have regular checkups. I'm doing everything I can to stay healthy."

"Ah, the vegetables, the workouts." Belo nodded as if a mystery had been solved. "But if you are working toward health, if you have learned more of what matters most, then why do you not wish to have love in your life?"

Lucas sucked in a breath. Now or never. "Belo, I... the treatments were hard on me. I don't know if—" He broke off and swallowed.

Belo simply tilted his head, watching Lucas.

"I don't know if I can father children. Sometimes, from what I've read and heard, fertility can be compromised, so..." He trailed off.

And watched the light die out of his grandfather's eyes.

In no way was he prepared to have this conversation. "Look, Belo, it's not all about bloodlines. You've had an influence on many young people. You're influencing Tyrone and Roscoe right now."

Belo nodded, his shoulders slumping. "I find I am feeling tired," he said. "Could we..." He gestured toward the door.

"Of course." Lucas stood and went to Belo's side, helping him up. "Let's get you home."

Belo shuffled out of the bakery on Lucas's arm and walked to the car. Lucas opened the passenger door and Belo got in silently.

The drive home was silent, too. But when they pulled up to the house, Belo put a hand on Lucas's arm as he turned off the car. "I want you well. I had not thought... that I could... lose you." His breathing was labored.

"I'm working my hardest to get well," Lucas said. "I promise, I'll keep doing that. It's just... I can't do the other thing. Get married. Not with a young woman who wants a family."

"We will talk," Belo said. "Now, I need to rest."

After he'd gotten Belo settled and made an excuse for why he couldn't eat lunch with the family, Lucas went out and drove. Too fast. But he couldn't escape the demons in his head.

Was he going to die? Was the family line going to end with his life?

Did that matter?

He didn't know how he ended up at the church. Once there, he didn't have the energy to get out of the car, nor to drive away. Instead, he sat in the empty parking lot, looked at the simple cross on the church's steeple, and tried to pray.

Back when Lucas had been struggling alone with the worst of the chemo and radiation, one of the hospital orderlies had befriended him and talked to him about Christ. It had been something different from the way he'd grown up, attending mass but never really paying a lot of mind to his own relationship with the Lord.

He remembered Talib's warm eyes and confident demeanor, his long dreadlocks waving with the intensity of his talk about what God had done for him, how faith had changed his life. Talib had shown Lucas dozens of passages in the gospels about Jesus healing people with all sorts of ailments, physical and emotional. He'd taken Lucas's hand, held it, and told him he believed that God could heal him.

Lucas's own faith hadn't been nearly as strong, just a seed, really, but those days were when it had taken hold. He'd read the passages on healing over and over again, and he'd come to believe that if the Lord wanted to save him, he could.

He'd also promised to use whatever remaining life God bestowed on him to do good in the world. Oh, not like a preacher, Lucas didn't have that in him. But through his work, he hoped to reach people, improve their health, lift up their emotional state.

He hadn't considered at the time that part of healing and helping might be about people like Belo and the boys and yes, like Veronica. But he did know that God didn't rule out a surprise or two along life's way.

Lucas had told Belo the truth today and it had hurt him. But at least Belo knew the situation now. He knew why Lucas couldn't pursue Veronica and form a family with her.

He should have felt relieved, but all he felt was empty.

"I'm sorry I'm not a good Christian, Father. Is that why you struck down the last of our line?" He lifted his face to feel the lowering sun warm it.

The force of the answer he received pressed him back into the seat of his car. Not words, but a vibration and a pressure, and Lucas knew without having to think about it exactly what was meant.

Fruitfulness and continuation in the world wasn't about biological parenthood. It was about faith, and spreading it. Radical trust in God, who'd made every person and every blade of grass.

So he might not father children, probably wouldn't. But he'd pass life lessons along to the boys, Tyrone and Roscoe. He'd help Belo through his golden years, sharing love, showing his grandfather that the years he'd devoted to his family meant something and that he had someone to care about him.

And Veronica, Lord?

No answer.

"What about Veronica?" he asked aloud. If God was going to offer earth-shaking insights on a number of topics, why couldn't he include an understanding of the woman who'd invaded Lucas's senses and turned upside down his ideas of right and wrong, of love and friendship? What did God have in mind for them?

Wait.

He sighed as the insight came to him, maybe from God, probably so. He had to wait. He couldn't know the outcome of their relationship now, couldn't know what it might mean.

He had a guess, though. Just like Paul had a thorn in the flesh, something that bothered him and couldn't be cured, something that made him rely on God, maybe Lucas was being tested by his attraction to Veronica.

He wanted her, heart and soul. In the quiet of the churchyard, he could admit it. The more he saw of her, the more he appreciated her wisdom and caring, all wrapped up in the playful form of a young woman for whom life hadn't yet become wearisome.

The way she'd charmed Belo. The sweet care with which she related to her abuela. The openness with which she'd accepted two loud, messy, troubled teen boys into her sphere of influence. No matter how annoying they became, she tried to keep it positive and cheerful, and her impact was obvious every time she walked into the kitchen or welcomed them home from work. And yeah, maybe the cookies fragrant in the oven were from a plastic tube at the grocery store, but for those two boys, it was some of the best mothering they'd ever experienced.

Lucas had to acknowledge being with her was sweet torture, because he wanted more, wanted to pin it down and make it permanent, this sprout of love that was growing between them.

Yet clutching it tightly, clutching it at all, would kill it.

And trying to tie Veronica to him, whether through her innocent attraction or through some sense of obligation, would be absolutely wrong.

A part of him, the cowardly part, wanted to send her on her way. To get her out of his immediate circle so he wouldn't have to see what he couldn't have.

But God didn't ask anyone, Lucas included, to take the easy road. Having Veronica around was a pain that ached more for the sweetness.

So he prayed the only prayer he could: *Help me to bear it.*

10

When Veronica arrived home from visiting a girlfriend that evening, the house wasn't the buzzing beehive of activity she'd come to expect. Instead, the place was silent.

Belo was in his room and, according to the boys, refused to come out. Lucas was working outside, his face grim, digging a garden and waving aside offers of help.

Abuela sat in the kitchen with Tyrone and Roscoe, all three faces glum.

The boys, at least, perked up when Veronica walked in. "What's for dinner?" Roscoe asked.

"I thought Lucas was going to cook for you," she countered. "What happened?"

"He told us to order pizza."

"And? Did you?"

"That's not a proper meal," Abuela said, "so we waited for you to come home."

Something was off here, but having been raised in a restaurant family, Veronica knew that the first step was food. "We'll order takeout from Fire and Brimstone," she decided. "Abuela, it *is* real food, and healthy food. If you haven't had it yet, you'll see.

We'll get three different kinds of pizza. Boys, find the menu online so we can order."

Meanwhile, she was pulling lettuce, snap peas, carrots, radishes, and tomatoes out of the fridge. "I'll make us a nice salad to have while we're waiting, and you can tell me what's wrong."

Fifteen minutes later, the four of them were sitting around the table eating salad, even the boys, with some degree of gusto.

"Belo wouldn't come down?" she asked Tyrone.

He swallowed a huge mouthful of greens. "He told me to go away."

"And Lucas?" she asked Roscoe. She was proud of how she kept her tone of voice the same when asking about the grandson as when asking about the grandfather.

She couldn't forget that kiss they'd shared, even though it had been brief. The feel of his stubbly face, the touch of his lips, the warm feeling of his arms around her, all of it was etched in her heart, and she found herself reliving it at the most inconvenient times.

Unfortunately, she spent even more time remembering what he'd said. "It won't happen again. I have my own good reasons for staying unencumbered."

He'd said she should marry, but just not him.

Any man who was willing to see a woman marry someone else, didn't really care for that woman. She had to get her head around that. Lucas saw her as a friend, an employee, someone he mentored.

Not as someone to explore a relationship with.

Her plans of using him to learn how to be in a relationship had backfired, because her feelings had grown. And his hadn't.

"Lucas says he's going to get the garden dug before sunset, and that we should eat without him," Roscoe said. "He's in a bad mood, too."

Abuela shook her head. "That is not good. A man should have his dinner, or the bear will bite."

"He about bit my head off," Roscoe said. "He doesn't know how to have fun, that's for sure."

"Okay, listen," Veronica said. She couldn't have a relationship with Lucas, but she could care for him and his grandfather as the friends they were. "I'm going to drive into town and pick up the pizzas. You guys have to find a way to get the men in here. We'll plan something fun."

On the way into town, and then back with the steaming, fragrant pizzas on the seat beside her, Veronica tried to talk herself into a better mood.

It was actually good that Lucas refused to be in a relationship with her, because that way, she wouldn't be derailed from her goals of independence. Her feelings for him were part and parcel of her problem:. She'd grown up with her older brothers taking care of her problems, and it was natural for her to fall for a man so similar to them.

She needed to learn to stand on her own two feet.

And she needed to be able to be around successful, older, alpha males without coming under their spell... lest it lead to the kind of situation she'd faced in Twin Falls, where the older man in question didn't have her good at heart.

So she'd try to figure out a way to be around Lucas without it being awkward and without it being romantic. Instead, they'd be friends. And instead of him taking control, she'd take some of the control, making it a more normal friendship and relationship.

When she arrived back at Belo's place and went inside, the three pizza boxes in her hands, a gloomy scene awaited her.

Belo was there, a robe over his thin, old-man pajamas, slippers on his feet, his normally neat face covered with grey stubble. He seemed to have aged ten years in the past day.

Definitely something for a doctor to look into. Maybe even her brother Daniel. Sure, he was a chiropractor, but his overall medical knowledge was excellent. A plan started to formulate in her mind.

Lucas was there in his work clothes; in fact she almost tripped over his work boots, muddy in the doorway. He leaned on one elbow, heavy and silent.

Abuela was obviously trying to make conversation, but the boys had gotten tongue-tied at the silence of their elders and it was an uphill battle.

"Food's here!" she called, making her voice cheerful. "Tyrone, you get plates, and Roscoe, you get out glasses and pour everyone some iced tea or lemonade. We'll pray and then everyone can get their own, because we've got three very different kinds."

Once the table was set, Veronica looked at Belo. "Would you pray for us?"

The old man lifted an eyebrow, but she kept her eyes on his, letting a pleading little smile creep onto her face. "Please?"

He sighed, nodded, and bowed his head, reaching out to clasp Abuela's hand on one side and Lucas's on the other. Veronica quickly sat down between the two boys, knowing they wouldn't want to hold each other's hands.

Belo offered a simple prayer, and then they all filed by the boxes. The uniqueness of the offering raised everyone's spirits a little, and once they were all digging in, conversation about the unusual pizza started up.

When it flagged, Veronica turned to Lucas. "What's going on with the garden?"

He shrugged. "I needed a project."

"Like the book isn't enough?" she asked.

"This one," Belo said, "does not know how to stop working." He put a hand on Lucas's shoulder and squeezed.

"That's what I want to talk to all of you about," Veronica said. "I need a day off, and I think everyone else does too. Let's all go do something fun together."

"Like what?" Tyrone sounded skeptical.

"No offense," Roscoe added, "but what's fun for you old folks isn't necessarily fun for us."

Veronica wavered between dismay that the boy had obviously included her and Lucas among the old folks, and pleasure that he was united with Tyrone as an 'us.' "There are things that are fun for all ages," she argued.

"Like what?" Tyrone asked again.

Veronica looked around at Lucas, Belo, and Abuela. "Help me out here," she said.

Abuela frowned thoughtfully. "There is a spring festival in Twin Falls."

"Shopping and walking around," Roscoe said flatly. "I've been to them with my mom. No way."

"And I'm afraid I would not be able to walk around so much," Belo said apologetically.

"Any hobbies, then?"

"Everyone can help me garden," Lucas said.

All of them groaned. "That's not relaxing, that's doing another hard project," Veronica pointed out.

"I have an idea," Belo said unexpectedly. "Fishing."

"Fishing?" Veronica asked, feeling doubtful.

Lucas grinned for the first time all evening. "Belo is quite the fisherman. I remember him taking me out when I was a kid. But —" He turned to his grandfather. "Won't that be a little much for you now?"

Belo shook his head. "There is no more fishing the fast streams off the beaten path for me," he said, "but fishing at the lake, with a chair and a picnic..."

"That's my kind of fishing," Abuela said, her eyes sparkling. "I used to go for the day with..." She looked over at Belo and stopped speaking, her cheeks going pink. "With friends," she said primly.

"What do you boys think?" Veronica asked.

Tyrone shrugged. "I've never been."

"Me either," Roscoe said.

"Never been fishing? Then we have to go!" Veronica looked at each of them. "We'll see which of you catches the first fish and the biggest one," she added, sensing that some competition would motivate them.

"Everyone has to bait their own hook." Lucas looked at her with laughter in his eyes.

She smiled back. "No problem for me."

Something electric sparked between them.

"If I even decide to fish," she added hastily, looking away from him. "I might read a book instead."

"I'll clean up," Lucas said, and stood.

"And I would like a small glass of port before bed," Belo said. "Would the *Señora* care to join me?" he added, holding out an arm to Abuela.

Her cheeks went pink as she accepted his arm, and Veronica raised an eyebrow. The connection between her grandmother and Belo was obvious.

The boys stuffed the remaining pizza in their mouths and rushed from the room. Lucas looked after them, his mouth opening, then closed it ruefully and looked at Veronica. "I could chase after them and make them help," he said.

"Or, since it'll take about two minutes, we could just do it ourselves."

He nodded. "It'll give us a chance to talk."

LUCAS WATCHED Veronica put away the remaining pizza and thought about what to say.

His prayers hadn't given him any answers, but he knew he had to be appropriate with Veronica, not create any unrealistic expectations. "About tomorrow," he said.

She half turned toward him. "Yeah?"

"Come outside," he said, "I'll get the dishes later."

She hesitated, and then followed him out into the sunset. "Show me your garden project," she said.

"Sure." He led her over toward the newly-turned earth. "I want to grow my own vegetables, pesticide free, like Beatriz does," he said.

"Good idea, though a lot of work."

"I have two laborers," he joked while trying to figure out how to say what he needed to say.

"The boys?"

He nodded. The sun was sinking down below the horizon, turning the fields and bluffs a fiery pinkish red. From the newly-turned earth came a rich, fertile smell. The breeze lifted a strand of Veronica's hair and blew it across her face, and Lucas had to fist his hand to keep from reaching out to pull it back for her.

Now or never. "I'm glad we're all going fishing tomorrow, but I wanted to clarify that I'm not wanting to build a family with you."

She tilted her head to one side. "Build a ... what?"

"Build a family. I mean, have a relationship. I mean...."

Her mouth twisted a little. "You think that going fishing with this group is going to make me want to marry you?"

"No, no, when you put it like that..."

"Or give me some kind of crazy expectations? Lucas." She put a hand on his arm and then snatched it back. "Sorry, I didn't mean anything by that."

And she didn't need to know that her touch felt like fire.

"Look, I... I'm sorry about that kiss. Heat of the moment, just a mistake, didn't mean anything. I'm not looking for that and I'm not interested in a relationship with someone like you, anyway."

Lucas's heart turned over. "Someone like me." Did she know about the cancer?

"I mean... It's just, I need to meet men who are... different. Younger. Not as..." She broke off, flushing.

Wow. Okay. He'd asked for this by bringing this discussion out into the open, he supposed. He shouldn't be shocked that it hurt. "Great, then, that's great," he said.

"Lucas, I'm sorry, I meant no offense." Again she touched his arm, and again she pulled back her hand quickly. "I like you, I really do. And I think this project we're working on is awesome, and we'll have a fantastic time tomorrow. I just don't want anything more, you know?"

"Then we're on the same page," he said firmly.

11

S he could do this, Veronica told herself firmly as she helped Lucas unload the SUV. She could do a day at the lake without getting overly romantic feelings about the tall, brawny, intelligent man beside her.

She grabbed a giant picnic basket and tried to pull it out of the car.

"Whoa, let me help you with that." Lucas grabbed the other handle. "It's heavy."

"I can do it."

"Let me be the man," he said, a smile tilting the corner of his mouth upwards.

She couldn't help smiling back at him. "Okay. You be the man."

Maybe she *couldn't* get through a day without romantic feelings.

"Hey, Lucas, the minnows are getting out!" Roscoe knelt beside the bait bucket, where a couple of tiny minnows flipped and thrashed.

"Way cool!" Tyrone came over, his usual swagger overcome by common boyish enjoyment of slimy creatures, and together, the two boys caught the escaped baitfish and returned them to the bucket. When Roscoe dove for a particularly antsy straggler, caught it, and tossed it into the bait bucket, Tyrone fist-bumped him. Then they picked up the bucket and fishing rods and followed Belo toward the lake.

"I can't believe they're getting along." Lucas murmured as he pulled out another folding canvas chair and then slammed the hatch of the SUV and locked it.

"That's what fishing and nature can do for you, I guess." She smiled up at him. And then, precisely because her eyes wanted to linger, she looked away, focusing back on the boys.

Belo was talking to them now, his voice soothing and rhythmic. The three got set up at a picnic table beside the lake, Tyrone and Roscoe helping Belo into a comfortable, sturdy lawn chair.

"This is how you hook them," she heard Belo say, holding a fishing pole and demonstrating to the boys.

Lucas put a hand on Veronica's arm, stopping her. For a foolish moment she thought he was feeling romantic, too, but he nodded toward the others. "He did that for me when I was a kid," he said as they watched the old man help the two boys to bait their hooks. "Nice to see him finding a new audience."

"A pretty attentive one, from the looks of things." As they walked toward the trio, Veronica was just as happy as Lucas was to watch them having fun together. Then Belo cast out, his line arcing perfectly over the water despite his sitting position.

"It's all in the wrist," Lucas said at the same time Belo did. The two grinned at each other, and Veronica sucked in her breath to see the family resemblance—and the family love—so strong between them.

Lucas helped Roscoe and Tyrone cast, then looked at Veronica. "You're fishing too, right?"

"Do I have to?" She looked at him from underneath the brim

of her sunhat. She really just wanted to relax. And chill. And watch Lucas with his grandfather and the boys. The sight of the three generations—especially the sight of Lucas—made tenderness warm her heart.

Man, she had it bad.

She reached into her bag for her library book and held it up. "I'm just gonna read for a little while and leave you men to your manly tasks," she joked.

Lucas came over to help her set up her chair. "Are you sure you won't be bored? I'm sorry your grandma couldn't come and keep you company."

Veronica nodded. "Me, too, but I don't think either of us is as disappointed as your grandfather."

"Yeah." Lucas frowned. "The two of them have gotten pretty close. Surprising, since they've been enemies for most of their lives."

"What's that saying? There's a fine line between love and hate."

"You may be right," he said, his eyes lingering on her face, "but how do you know so much about love?"

I know nothing. She ducked under her hat. It was all too easy to slide into a flirty, teasing relationship with Lucas, but he'd made it clear he didn't want that. She wasn't going to throw herself at him.

She was going to learn to stand on her own two feet if it killed her.

"What are you reading?" Lucas knelt beside her.

She held out the book, her cheeks heating. "*Successfully Single.* It's about how our culture encourages all of us to fall in love and couple up, when really, some people are made to be alone."

He frowned at her. "You don't put yourself in that category, do you?"

Did she? She'd always thought she'd marry and raise a family, when she was a kid. But now, now that she was older and saw the way of the world a little more, she wondered. "I don't know. I like men, and I like the idea of family. But I find it hard to be involved with someone without getting engulfed. And I know for sure that I need to figure out who I am apart from my brothers."

"Don't you already know who you are?" He moved closer and looked up at her, making it so she couldn't hide beneath the brim of her hat. "You seem pretty grounded for as young as you are."

"I don't want to cut off my opportunities to explore too soon," she said. "And I don't want to make any mistakes in relationships, like some of my friends have done. I already know two of my college buddies are getting divorced."

"Awful." Lucas shook his head. " "I've seen a lot of that, too."

"Our grandparents' generation had something on ours," she said. "You stuck with each other, worked things out. There's not much of that anymore."

"I believe in it, though," he said.

Again, their eyes caught and held.

"My parents had such a happy—"

A loud splash from the direction of Belo and the boys interrupted her comment, and she stood quickly to see what was happening.

"Roscoe!" Lucas was already running toward the dock, and Veronica followed behind him.

In the few seconds it took the two of them to arrive, Roscoe surfaced from the lake to the sound of Tyrone's and Belo's laughter.

Veronica ignored it. "Are you okay? What happened?"

"Just showing off," he said, splashing back to the shore, where he started to shiver.

"You looked like a fool, man!" But Tyrone's insult sounded friendly rather than hostile.

"Come on." Lucas clapped a hand on the boy's shoulder. "You need to change out of those wet clothes."

"I didn't bring anything else to wear."

"There's always spare stuff in my car." He guided the boy toward the SUV and they disappeared from view behind the open hatch.

When they came back over, Roscoe now wearing a sweatshirt and flannel pants that must belong to Lucas, Veronica realized the boy looked a bit slimmer than he had the previous week. And his face was a bit more relaxed as well.

"Dude, you look ridiculous," Tyrone said, again without rancor.

"Still better than you, shrimp." Roscoe bumped Tyrone's shoulder as he walked back to the bait bucket.

Belo and Lucas exchanged a couple of sentences in Spanish, too low for Veronica to catch. "Are you sure?"

"*Sí, sí,* I am sure." Belo pushed himself out of his chair and beckoned to the boys, and the three of them headed down to the next dock, Tyrone holding out his arm for Belo to steady himself.

"He's going to show them how to clean fish," Lucas said, leaning back against the railing along the side of the dock. "Even though they've only caught one so far. Which means he's trying to leave us alone to make something happen."

"Make something happen? What do you mean?"

Lucas pointed at her and then at himself. "Between us. Make something happen between us."

Veronica felt her cheeks heat as she looked away from Lucas's face to Belo's departing back. "Why does he still want something... to happen... between us?" She wished she sounded calm, cool, and collected instead of breathless.

Lucas didn't answer, and after a minute she hazarded a glance back at him.

His hand was on his upper back, his body twisted oddly. He clutched the railing hard.

"Are you okay?" Veronica asked, all flirtatious notions vanishing instantly, replaced by concern. "What's wrong?"

"I think... could you get me something to drink?" Lucas's face had gone pale.

"Sure! Just a minute!" She ran to the mini-cooler she'd set up by her reading chair, grabbed a bottle of water, and ran back toward the dock, where Lucas was now sitting down on a bench.

She knelt beside him and unscrewed the bottle cap. "Are you sick?"

"I didn't think so but..." He paused and drank deeply. "I might need to go to the hospital." He didn't sound surprised; more like resigned.

"To the hospital!" Veronica stared at him. "What... are you sure? Should I call an ambulance?"

"No," he said, wincing again. "I know what this is. I've been trying to ignore some minor symptoms but..." He tried to stand, then collapsed back down, holding onto the dock's railing.

What was wrong? She wasn't used to seeing Lucas as anything but strong and competent. "I'll get the boys to help get you to the car."

"No. No... time. I can do it." He heaved himself up, and she put out a hand and steadied him. Then she held his arm as they turned toward the car.

She walked beside him slowly, holding his arm, her mind racing. He didn't want an ambulance, and truthfully, she could probably drive him faster to the hospital herself. "Do you have the car keys?"

"In... my pocket." He nearly fell, catching himself at the last minute on the edge of the picnic table and easing himself down.

He managed to get out the car keys and dropped them into her hand.

"Stay there." Veronica rushed ahead of him to open the door and slide back the passenger seat as far as it would go. Then she rushed back to the picnic table. He looked even more pale now, and his upper lip shone with fine beads of sweat.

She walked him slowly to the car and used all her strength to help him into the passenger seat. She buckled him in and closed the door.

Grabbing a passing woman's arm, she pointed out Belo and the boys, and asked her to relay a message. And then she drove like a maniac to the hospital, stuffing down all the questions she wanted to ask Lucas, who was leaning back against the headrest, his eyes closed.

In the ER, they set Lucas up with an IV and pulled up his records, and only then did they look at Veronica. "What's your relationship?" a stern nurse asked.

His eyes fluttered open. "She's... my wife. He reached out and clutched Veronica's hand.

Veronica blinked at the lie, but saw the reason for it. "I won't leave you."

He smiled a little, thanking her with eyes that looked large against his pale face.

She squeezed his hand and tried to look steady and mature and wife-like for the nurse, but inside she was shaking, her heart pounding. What did all this mean? What was wrong with Lucas? She didn't want to ask the question of the busy medical professionals who were examining Lucas, so she texted her brother Daniel, the chiropractor, and told him the symptoms.

At which point she learned that Daniel knew things about Lucas's medical condition, had guessed them at least, but hadn't seen fit to tell her. "I couldn't. Still can't. It's confidential."

"The man practically passed out at the lake!" Veronica

pounded the letters into her phone, so great was her frustration. If she was living on Lucas's property, working as his assistant, she needed to know that kind of thing, but neither Daniel nor Lucas had told her.

She knew why. They thought she was a young, incompetent female, worthy of protection but not of being a mature peer.

"Ma'am," one of the nurses said, "we're taking him to a room."

"More later," she texted and then turned off the phone.

The next hour was a flurry of tests and consultations. Once they were finally alone in the room, awaiting results of all the tests, Veronica sat on the edge of the bed. "Do you feel well enough to talk?"

He nodded. "I couldn't sleep if my life depended on it."

"Then Lucas, you have to tell me. What's the matter with you?"

He sighed, looked away from her at the blank wall, and then turned back to meet her eyes. "I have a rare form of spinal cancer. Stage 3."

Veronica stared as pain and sympathy twisted her heart. "You have something that serious and you didn't tell me?" Her throat tightened on the last words. Not because he hadn't told her, but because he was suffering through this pain all alone.

And because, stage three... Wow. She didn't even want to go into what that meant, what the survival rate might be. Imagining the world without Lucas had become impossible for her, just in the few short weeks they'd worked together.

"Almost nobody knows," he said. "Around here, it's only your brother Daniel—he guessed, he doesn't know details—and Belo. Speaking of whom—"

"My brothers are going out to get them at the lake, don't worry," she said quickly. "They'll figure out how much to tell them and make sure they're okay at home. But Lucas, how can you carry this burden all alone?" She reached out and rubbed his arm, gently, soothingly, as she'd do for a child.

He shrugged and shifted in the hospital bed. "I've been doing it for years. It's better than when people pity you."

"How many years?"

"Three," he said.

"And you dealt with it all alone, away from your home and family?"

"Not at first." He sighed. "Veronica, this isn't common knowledge, but I was married up until six months ago."

"You... you were married?" That hit her like a blow to the chest. "How come nobody knows about it?"

He shook his head. "I wasn't married in the church, so Belo wouldn't have acknowledged it. And I couldn't tell him, because the idea of me marrying outside the church, well, it would have broken his heart."

"And you're divorced now?" Her view of Lucas's life was undergoing significant changes, and she felt like she was asking the questions by rote, not able to make complete sense of what he was saying. "Is this your secret? All of this?"

He nodded. "I had to tell Belo about the cancer, or rather, it just slipped out. But I don't want it to be common knowledge."

"Is that why you don't want to have a relationship with me?" she asked with sudden insight.

He nodded. "Even if you wanted to be with someone older, like me—and I don't take that for granted, not at all—it wouldn't be fair to you. I may never have children. I may not even live to see my fortieth birthday."

She absolutely could not deal with that concept, so she shut that last remark out. "What happened between you and your wife?"

He adjusted his hospital bracelet, took a drink of water from the plastic tumbler by his bed. "She tried. I don't want to put any blame on her, because she stood by me for two years, while things were at their worst. It was only when my chances started to improve that she..." He broke off, shrugged.

"She left you then?" That didn't add up, not to Veronica anyway.

He nodded. "She was too loyal to leave me when I was flat on my back, going through chemo and radiation. But when my treatments got further apart and I was going to come home full time, she let me know that it wasn't working for her."

Ouch. Still trying to process his story, Veronica didn't speak. She just shifted off his bed and pulled up a chair to sit beside him.

He looked at her steadily for a couple of minutes. "We'd had trouble before," he said. "She didn't like my lifestyle of constant travel, even though that was how I'd met her. And she was young. Too young to deal with having a sick husband, with the uncertainty of not knowing whether the cancer would come back."

Veronica blew out a breath. She got it. Knowing that your husband's fate was constantly in question would be difficult, akin to being married to a soldier or police officer or firefighter.

"So you've sworn off relationships now." She heard the flat sound in her own voice and didn't know where it had come from. Maybe from shock.

She was trying to figure out what to ask next when the hospital room's door opened.

"Mr. Ruiz?" asked a doctor with short, salt-and-pepper hair and wire-rimmed glasses.

"That's me." Lucas sat forward, his hand clenching the railing of the hospital bed.

The doctor glanced from him to Veronica and back, then frowned. "I'm afraid I have some bad news."

12

Lucas already felt like he'd been hit by a truck. But the doctor's words threatened something more like a fall over a cliff.

He glanced over at Veronica. "You should leave."

"No." Deliberately she moved closer and put her hand on top of his. "I'm your wife," she said, loud enough for the doctor to hear. "I want to hear everything."

Emotions roiled through him. Sadness and loss, because Tara had been like that when she'd first learned of his illness. Longing, to have a soul mate at his side who truly supported him, on whom he could rely. Embarrassment, because he was supposed to be the strong one.

The doctor glanced back at his chart and lifted an eyebrow. "So.... you've married since your last exam?"

Veronica gripped his hand tighter. "Yes, he has. We're keeping it a secret, though, so it's not in your records."

"All right, if it's okay with you, Lucas, I'll talk with your... wife, in the room."

He looked at Veronica one more time and kissed goodbye

the dreams he'd had of a carefree relationship with her. Once she heard the worse, she'd run, just as Tara had.

But that was as it should be. He'd not shackle another woman with his issues. "It's fine," he said. "Tell me."

TEN MINUTES LATER, his head was spinning. And aching pretty badly, so the doctor had ordered some pain medication and rest.

Veronica looked as shell-shocked as he felt. And no wonder. Before today, he'd been her boss and an acquaintance, maybe somewhat of a friend. Even someone with whom she was carrying on a light flirtation.

Now, she'd learned that his case might be terminal.

That was a pretty bad shocker when you first learned of it. It was a shocker now, even though he'd heard the words before.

His cancer had more than likely returned. For the first time since his chemo had ended, the blood markers were going in the wrong direction. And while the doctor had emphasized that the test results had only a 2/3 accuracy rate, the fact that he'd gotten sharp pains in his back, that he'd suddenly weakened and nearly passed out was, as the doctor had said, worrisome.

"You should go," he said to Veronica, trying to extract his hand from hers. He had to give her credit, she'd sat right there and listened to the medical jargon without flinching and without letting go of his hand. She'd even asked a few questions for clarification, something Tara had never managed to do.

Veronica didn't let go of his hand. Instead, she leaned forward and rested her cheek on their joined knuckles. "Oh, Lucas," she said. "I'm so sorry you have this to deal with. What can I do to help?"

"Your being here was a help." It was true. Even though she wasn't his wife, and her caring couldn't be permanent, having Veronica there had softened the blow.

"I see now why you're so interested in the food-health connection," she said.

"Yes, although it'll be a challenge to finish the book and go through more treatments." He heard his own voice slurring and knew he didn't have long before the drugs kicked in. "Listen, Veronica, I'd appreciate if you kept this to yourself for now."

She frowned. "You don't want to go through this kind of thing alone," she said. "You have friends and family here in Arcadia Valley who will help you."

"It'll worry Belo."

"Well," she pointed out, "Belo is already worried. He's called me twice."

"That's what I don't want."

"You've got it, Lucas," she said flatly. "This is Arcadia Valley. The boys and Belo saw what happened, and my brothers got involved to help out. Like it or not, you're part of a community. And everyone wants to help you."

Everyone wants to help you. The words swirled around in his head as he lost his battle to stay awake.

And his feelings about those words—and about the concern in Veronica's eyes—yo-yoed back and forth with dizzying speed.

AFTER LUCAS FELL into what was obviously a deep and much-needed sleep, Veronica went out into the hall in search of a soda and some fresh air.

"Veronica!"

The sound of Javier's voice surprised her, and then it didn't. Of course he'd come, was even now beckoning to her.

And then her other two brothers emerged from the waiting room at the end of the hall. "You okay, Ronnie?" Alex asked, holding out his arms.

As she let him wrap her up in a big hug, Veronica felt

herself sag against him. The tension of trying to hold herself together in the face of this shocking news, to be the strong one, released suddenly, and she had to blink against sudden tears.

She swallowed hard. No way was she going to let her brothers see how upset she was. "I'm fine," she said, and pulled back out of Alex's arms.

"How's Lucas?" Daniel asked, frowning. "I'd like to get in and talk to him."

"He's sleeping," she said. "But I know he'd like to talk to you. There was so much information to process. And by the way"—she glared at him "—thanks a lot for keeping his condition from me."

"What *is* his condition?" Javier asked. "I just heard he collapsed and you rushed him to the hospital."

Veronica looked at Daniel. "I can't tell them, can I?"

He lifted his hands, palms up. "His grandfather told Abuela, and the boys overheard and told a couple of friends. I'm actually surprised it didn't get back to you yet, Javier."

Javier looked distinctly guilty. "Well, as a matter of fact..."

"You know!" She put her hands on her hips and glared at him. "So why'd you act like you didn't? And how did you hear?"

"It was Nora," he admitted. "I guess the boys are friendly with her, and they were texting, and when Nora heard, she got freaked out and told Molly. I couldn't help overhearing."

Veronica sighed, glancing back at the closed door of Lucas's room. That was Arcadia Valley, the good and the bad of it. She wondered how Lucas would react to the whole town knowing his condition.

"I guess I'm the only one who doesn't know then," Alex said.

And he'd hear soon enough. "He has cancer in his spine," she said, "or had it, anyway, and the doctors think it might have recurred."

"Whoa." Alex whistled, shaking his head. "He's young for that."

"We never know what's facing us," Javier said. Then he took Veronica's hand and pulled her toward the lounge. "Still, you shouldn't be having to deal with all of this. You're his assistant, not a wife or a girlfriend."

"I can't let him go through it alone," she said. "He's become a friend, and he doesn't have anyone else."

Javier opened his mouth to protest and then closed it again.

"It's a lot to handle," Daniel said gently. "I respect you for wanting to be a friend, but if he's going to be going through a rough course of treatment, he's probably not going to be able to continue working on his book."

"Which means you'll be out of a job, kiddo." Alex sat down beside her and put an arm around her. "I'm sorry you're dealing with this."

"It's not me who's facing anything, really," she said. "It's him."

"And we should pray, first of all," Javier said, and Veronica was ashamed she hadn't thought of it before.

So the four Quintana siblings pulled chairs into a circle in the waiting room, held hands, and prayed.

VERONICA WAS READYING Lucas's room for his homecoming, making up the bed with Roscoe's help, when Tyrone came into the room.

"Did you ask her?" He directed the question at Roscoe.

"Not yet," Roscoe said, ducking his head to ease a pillow into its pillowcase.

"Ask me what?" Veronica finished spreading the top sheet and began tucking it in at the foot of the bed.

The two boys looked at each other. "What's going to happen to us?"

Veronica blew out a breath. "The truth is, I don't know," she said. "I'm not a guardian for either of you, of course; Lucas is. Not officially, not for you, Roscoe, but your aunt left you in Lucas's care."

"And he's real sick," Roscoe said. "Aunt Connie wants me to come home, but..."

"Oh, man, don't go. If you go, I'll have to go, too." The vulnerability in Tyrone's voice illustrated how far he'd come. He wasn't playing tough anymore, but pleading with Roscoe to help him keep this place to stay.

Veronica looked at Tyrone. "Have you let your family know about the change of situation?" she asked.

"No." He snorted out a laugh. "They don't care."

Veronica put an arm around him for a quick squeeze, knowing he wouldn't accept more, thinking of her three older brothers. She resented their interference in her life at times, but she was blessed. "I don't know what will happen," she said, "but if you both want to stay, I'm game to help you. You'll have to work more around the house, though. And if Lucas needs help, with moving, showering, that sort of thing, it might be that you guys will have to get involved with it."

"I've helped my mom a lot," Roscoe said. "I used to lift her into the bathtub."

"Dude!" Tyrone cringed.

Roscoe shrugged philosophically. "It's what you do when somebody's sick."

"I'm grossed out by sick people," Tyrone admitted. "But I can do other stuff. Help with his garden, or go to the market."

She squeezed his shoulder. "We'll all work together, and Belo and Abuela will help, too. We'll try to get Lucas better."

Inside, she was quaking a little. By default, she'd become the coordinator of Lucas's care. The hospital staff still thought she was his wife. And although Belo had gone to see Lucas at the hospital, he'd needed a ride and was fighting his own health battles. He wasn't well enough to provide more than emotional support for his grandson.

Abuela was strong and healthy, but she was in her eighties. Veronica couldn't expect her to get more involved. She'd already helped plenty by providing Veronica with a listening ear and cooking advice.

No, the bulk of his care fell on her, and so it was with nervous anxiety that she heard the sound of the vehicle below.

Lucas. And her brothers, because Javier and Daniel had insisted on being the ones to bring him home.

They helped him inside, and his face was grey with the exertion. "Man, six days in the hospital, and I'm as weak as a newborn," he said as Daniel and Javier helped him to the couch.

"Do you want to go right to bed?" Veronica asked.

"No. I'll sit up awhile, because we have to talk."

Veronica shook her head. "Any talking that happens can wait until you're stronger."

"No," he said. "We'd best talk now." He glanced over at Javier.

"Veronica," her oldest brother said, "we think it's best if you move back home with me."

13

The next morning, Lucas woke up to the smell of coffee. When he opened his eyes, he saw that a tray with coffee, fruit, and whole-grain toast was sitting beside his bed.

Whoever had brought it was nowhere to be seen. Had the visiting nurse been here already?

There was an ache in his chest that had nothing to do with physical illness. Nor with fears about his future. He was old friends with the knowledge that his time on this earth might be limited.

No, it had to do with Veronica. Veronica, who'd helped him get to the hospital and then returned and gotten him set up at home when that was none of her responsibility. It showed maturity and kindness and even a special emotion for him. Something that might have grown into love, if he'd been extraordinarily blessed and if his health situation had been different.

But things weren't going to turn out that way, and so it was for the best that Veronica had moved back in with her brother. She didn't have any obligation to him, and to have her sacrifice herself because her employer was ill made no sense.

He'd known it himself, and her brothers had cemented the thought.

But even though he knew it was right, he felt an emptiness inside. Going through cancer alone just plain stunk. And he didn't know quite how he'd manage it. The social worker at the hospital had arranged for a visiting nurse, but long term, he'd have trouble paying for that.

Not to mention that most of the nurses in the area had been turned away by Belo. The Ruiz household had a reputation already.

He leaned over to get the coffee, joggled and spilled some, and in trying to clean it up, came upon his old Spanish-English New Testament.

He picked it up and wiped coffee from the cover, and then realized some had seeped inside. He opened it and blotted at what he now realized was a concordance, listing topics and where in the Bible to find them.

He skimmed the page, and a topic jumped out at him: Healing.

The same material he'd studied when he'd grown closer to God two years ago.

Getting comfortable, sitting up in the bed, he looked at the listed verses and then flipped to one he was familiar with from before. *While the sun was setting, all those who had any who were sick with various diseases brought them to Him; and laying His hands on each one of them, He was healing them.*

Sipping coffee, he read on through the book of Luke.

...The power of the Lord was present for Him to perform healing.

... He began speaking to them about the kingdom of God and curing those who had need of healing.

He fumbled for his note pad and computer and started copying verses down, soon going beyond the short concordance, searching the internet for "Jesus" and "healing" and "verses."

As he'd figured out before, and half forgotten, there were dozens.

What seemed like minutes later, there was a light tap on the door.

"Come in," he called, not looking up from his Bible.

"How are you doing?" The voice was sweet, familiar.

"Veronica?" He looked up and blinked. "You're here? Why? I thought..."

"I live here, silly." She came over and leaned into the side of his bed. "At least, I live in the cabin, but I seem to spend most of my time over here these days. You're not sick of me, are you?"

He set his computer aside to focus on her, make sure she wasn't a figment of his imagination. "Your brothers made you move home."

"My brothers don't control what I do." A smile tugged at the corner of her mouth.

He tilted his head to one side. "Veronica..."

"What?" Suppressed laughter made her eyes sparkle.

And he didn't need to focus on how pretty she was. "What kind of a fight did you put up to get Javier to let you stay?"

"It wasn't *too* bad once Abuela stepped in." And now her face broke out into a huge smile.

He tried hard not to return it, to shove aside the relief and gladness in his heart. "Javier is right this time," he said, making his voice firm. "You're a young woman with your whole future ahead of you. And for now, I'm a sick old man. You need to move on."

"But how would your book get written if I did that?"

He'd been worrying about the same thing, but it wasn't her problem. "The book is going on hold until I see how I'm feeling, how the remaining test results turn out and how much energy I have."

And whether it's true that Jesus can help me heal.

She shook her head. "If I'm here to help you," she said, "you can tell me what to do on the book and I can do it. We'll move forward. We'll even be able to test things out, some of the ideas about food healing cancer."

"You mean, test them out on me?"

"Uh-huh." She gestured toward the Bible in his hands. "Maybe God made all of this come together for a reason."

He looked at her for a long moment and she continued meeting his eyes, a peaceful expression on her face. He looked down at his Bible, and then back at her. The tiny seed of hope in his heart took root.

Outside the door, the sound of a vacuum cleaner roared, and then a crash. "What's going on? Belo's not cleaning, is he?"

She shook her head. "Nope. It's Tyrone. He's taken over the housekeeping. And when you need a man to help you with bathing or dressing, Roscoe is at your service."

"Roscoe?" Now he had to be hearing things. "Roscoe? He's a kid! They're both kids!"

She smiled. "They're teenagers, and Roscoe claims he's a decent nurse. Which is good, because I'm going to have my hands full with working on the book and helping Abuela with the cooking."

This was ridiculous. "What's Belo say about all of this?"

"Belo approves," she said. "In fact, he's been interviewing visiting nurses all morning. Claims that most of them are incompetent, but he's determined to find you a good one."

Lucas collapsed back against the pillows, his head spinning. A month ago, he'd been an independent, isolated man, making his solo way in life. Now, he was surrounded by a community of people helping him. Without his knowledge or consent.

"I don't know quite how to handle this," he said.

"You don't have to," she said. "Your job is to get well. Leave everything else to us."

"I'm TERRIFIED," Veronica admitted that evening at an emergency meeting of her prayer group.

Around her, murmurs of reassurance came from her friends: Charlotte Delis, Kate Groves, Maria Serrano, and Maria's mother, Mama Beatriz.

The home Maria shared with her mother, husband, and son was colorful and welcoming. Bright rugs covered the wood plank floors, and plants dominated the multiple windows, now letting in the afternoon sun. Maria's son, Tomasito, sat in the midst of the women, building towers of blocks and then knocking them over with loud shouts of "pow" and "boom" until Maria's husband came in and swooped the boy up into his arms. "Come on, *mijo,*" he said. "This is no place for us men. We're going to the park to run off some of this energy."

Maria reached up a hand to squeeze her husband's and a look of warmth and love passed between them. It made Veronica breathless with... what? Admiration? Envy?

She wanted what Maria had. Not just the husband, but the child as well.

And she wanted Lucas. But he'd already told her he might not have children. He might not even survive.

Pain twisted her stomach into knots.

Veronica had been coming to the Busy Women's Prayer Group for years. The membership fluctuated, and their agreement was that no one was to be made to feel guilty for not being able to join on any particular evening. If they didn't have time to cook and bring food, they ordered it from a local restaurant or made do with sandwiches and fruit.

The point was being together. At one time or another, each of them had struggled with something, and the group was there to cover them in prayer. It had been a blessing to Molly when she'd been new in town. It had helped Mama Beatriz through her chemo. And when Veronica had come back from Twin Falls, feeling terrible about herself and about what had happened, these women had prayed her through it.

"You're not obligated to take on the care of Lucas's household," Charlotte reminded her now. "It's a big job."

"From what I've heard," Maria said, "Lucas's grandfather is pretty wealthy. I'm sure they can afford to hire help."

"They could. They are. Belo is interviewing nurses to come in on a regular basis. And Lucas has a lot of support from his doctors. But..."

Mama Beatriz leaned forward and took Veronica's hand. "You want to be involved."

Veronica nodded. "Hired care isn't enough. He's got his grandfather, and his book, and the boys to take care of. I want to help him."

There was a tap on the door, and Molly came in. "Sorry I'm late, Maria. Is it okay that I let myself in?"

"Of course. Come sit down."

So much for being open and honest with her friends. Veronica loved Molly dearly, but Molly was loyal to Javier, as any woman would be to her husband. Which meant that whatever Veronica said here might get back to her big brother.

Molly shrugged out of her jacket and perched on the arm of the sofa. "What's going on?"

"Veronica just got some news about Lucas," Maria explained. "She's freaking out."

"His cancer? I heard. I think most people know by now."

That figured. Arcadia Valley wasn't exactly good at keeping secrets, especially if someone seemed to need help.

"So... catch me up. What have you guys been talking about?" Molly set the tray of bunuelos she'd brought on the coffee table. "Please, everyone, eat these so I don't."

"She's involved in taking care of him," Charlotte explained, "and she doesn't know if she can handle it."

"Neither does Javier," Molly said. "He wants you out of there. He thinks Lucas is taking advantage."

"Lucas wants me out of there, too!" Veronica threw up her hands. "Nobody thinks I can handle it, and everyone thinks I should just go back to being an extra hostess at El Corazon. It's so frustrating!"

"But it *is* a lot," Charlotte said gently. "You said so yourself. You said you were terrified."

"But being afraid doesn't mean I don't want to do it." Veronica looked around at her friends, beloved face to beloved face. "I need help and support, that's all. People to bounce ideas off of, who aren't going to jump in and take over like my brothers do."

"And we are here for you," Beatriz said in her soothing voice. "I for one applaud you for your Christian caring. But what of your heart, *mija?*"

"What do you mean?" Veronica shot an uneasy look at Molly, then at the other women.

"She means, why do you care so much," Molly said. "Why do you *want* to take care of Lucas? And—" She held up a hand. "Don't worry. What's said at prayer group stays at prayer group. I'm not going to run tattling to Javier."

"You're sure?" Veronica narrowed her eyes at Molly. Of course she meant well, but she and Javier told each other almost everything, as married couples should.

"Of course." Molly reached out to squeeze Veronica's hand. "I have a life apart from Javier, and I know how to keep a secret."

Veronica decided to trust her. "The truth is," she said, "I'm not sure why I care so much. Lucas is... different."

"Different from whom?" Mama Beatriz asked.

"I know who," Maria said, a twinkle in her eyes. "He's

different from the schoolboys Veronica usually hangs out with. Lucas is too smart to spend his time singing karaoke at the Legion."

"You mean he's a real, grown-up man?" quiet Kate asked.

"Yes!" Veronica looked around the room. "Lucas has been places and done things. He's successful. He knows how to take charge."

"Kind of like your brothers?" Molly said dryly.

"Well, yeah." Veronica stared down at her hands. "And that's a worry I have. Am I getting involved with someone like my brothers? Is that why I like Lucas so much?"

"Ladies." Mama Beatriz held up a hand, and they all turned to look at her, respecting her wisdom. She was a spiritual warrior and mentor to all of them. "The thing we can't lose track of is that Lucas is ill. That brings on a whole new amount of responsibility. It's not as if Veronica can just lightheartedly explore a new relationship with him, because he is in a life and death situation."

"And he was married before, and his wife couldn't handle his illness."

Everyone in the room looked shocked. "He was married?" Kate asked.

"I never heard that," Charlotte said.

"Can you handle it, Veronica?" Molly leaned forward. "I mean, you didn't stay at the job in Twin Falls very long. Seems like you're still finding your way, and this could derail you. I don't think you should get more involved with him unless you're really sure that that's the way you want to go."

Veronica bit her lip against the angry reply that wanted to come. Molly was right, after all. Although she didn't know the whole story of what had happened in Twin Falls, the truth was that Veronica hadn't been very good at handling it. Would she be any better at handling a boyfriend with a cancer diagnosis?

And what was this about a boyfriend? Lucas wasn't her boyfriend.

Maria glanced at her mother. "I'm not sure we have the wisdom in this room to handle the situation," she said. "But God knows what Veronica should do. I think we should turn to him."

"And that," Mama Beatriz said, "is the wisest thing we said tonight. Let's pray."

So they spent time asking for wisdom and insight for Veronica. Prayed for Lucas to be healed. And asked God to show his will for Veronica's life, whether she should stay, how much she should help Lucas, what should be done about the two young men in the household, and about Belo as well.

"Let's have a few moments of silent prayer," Maria said. "I feel like we all have questions to ask and that our Lord will reveal the answers more in silence."

So Veronica closed her eyes and begged the Lord for wisdom. She knew that taking care of others was what Jesus was all about. She knew that He healed the sick and expected each Christian to love their neighbors as themselves. All of that was clear, but what Veronica didn't know was whether her own desire to stay with Lucas, to be with him in his distress, was more about Christian caring or about Veronica's own needs. And if it had to do with her own needs, was that wrong? Were her own needs selfish, or had God put those needs into her?

After she had poured out all her questions to God, she sat in silence, and although she didn't feel definitive answers, slowly, a sense of peace came over her.

"Amen." Maria said the word quietly, and then looked around at the other women. "Does anyone want to speak up?"

"I do." Veronica looked around at each of them. "I still don't know what I'm going to do, but I know I can't do it alone. And I know I can't go running to my brothers when things go wrong.

I'm going to need support, and I hope you ladies will be here for me."

"Of course we will!" Molly came over and wrapped her arms around Veronica, and then the other women followed suit, putting hands on her shoulder and her back, hugging her and offering reassurance.

Soon the meeting broke up, and Veronica was headed out the door when Mama Beatriz beckoned to her. "Let me give you some vegetables and recipes," she said. "When Lucas interviewed me, I talked about the science, but Maria and I have the practical side covered, too. Concrete things you can do to help Lucas get well."

As Veronica followed Mama Beatriz and Maria back into their kitchen, she felt an overwhelming sense of rightness. Arcadia Valley was the right place to be, and this group of women was the support group she needed so that she could be a help to Lucas. She wasn't sure what God had in mind for the future, but for now, she would stay and take care of Lucas as best she could.

"Sit," Mama commanded. "I'm going to tell you some preliminary things to do for Lucas. But I want you to visit every week for a little more information, *si?*"

"If you don't mind, that would be wonderful."

"I like to spread the word of how eating fresh vegetables and whole grains and local fruits helped turn around my cancer," she said. "I certainly give credit to my doctors, too. And of course, most of the credit goes to the Lord, so you have to keep praying above anything else, for yourself and for Lucas. But in between those things, his diet should be a priority."

"Tell her about the smoothies," Maria urged, and the three of them bent over a handwritten list of recipes. Veronica took pictures with her phone, and by the time she left, she felt heartened.

There was something concrete she could do for Lucas. There were people who would help.

Thank you, Father.

When she got back to the hacienda, eager to share her new strength with Lucas and the rest of the household, she found only Belo, sitting disconsolate in the kitchen. "Lucas is gone," he said.

14

Had he done the right thing or made the worst mistake of his life?

Lucas sat in the Salt Lake City airport, waiting for his flight announcement. Pittsburgh. A smart place for a cancer patient to go. Far away from Arcadia Valley.

Away from all that love and caring and support, he could think. He could figure out what this recurrence in his cancer meant and what was next.

He could avoid causing pain to Belo, falsely raising the hopes of Tyrone and Roscoe.

He could stop falling in love with Veronica, and hopefully, keep her from falling in love with him.

"Attention, please. Flight 177, Direct to Pittsburgh, is ready to begin boarding at gate..."

Mechanically he stood and joined the cluster of people waiting to board. Many were with family groups, some having just enjoyed a western vacation, others heading east to visit relatives.

Not many, probably, were going away to escape family and community.

But he knew, from Tara, the toll that a cancer patient took on the lives of those close to him. He wasn't going to let that happen to the good people of Arcadia Valley.

Wasn't going to let it happen to Veronica.

The one person he'd confided in, Javier Quintana, had been in reluctant agreement with his decision, at least the version Lucas had shared. It was good to go where the cancer treatments were at their most modern. Good to limit the damage to his ailing grandfather, and Javier had agreed to look out for Belo as well as for Roscoe and Tyrone.

And Javier had been absolutely certain it was for the best for Lucas to leave before Veronica got more attached.

At the end of their conversation Javier had clapped him on the shoulder, then pulled him into an embrace. "You keep me updated and let me know what you need, man. It's not that I don't like you. I wouldn't even mind calling you brother—*cuñado*—if the circumstances were different."

But the circumstances weren't different, and here he was. Ready to start a new life.

He took one more look at the email he'd written to Veronica. That was the only thing he felt bad about, because he'd told a lie.

It was a white lie, and for her own good. It would hurt her, but it would also ensure that she didn't pine after him, but rather, went on with her promising young life.

But for just a moment, he thought of how she approached the computer each morning that they'd worked together. Smiling, laughing up at him, eager to see what mysteries and adventures her inbox might hold for today. Her squeal of delight at a note from an old friend or a sale at her favorite online clothing shop. Her ecstatic inhaling of the first cup of coffee before she took a sip.

Trying not to imagine her reaction when she opened this

particular email, he pushed away his own sense of loss and despair, whispered "I'm sorry," and hit "send."

"SHE HAS NOT GOTTEN out of her bed in two days."

Abuela's accented murmur penetrated the fog that had been surrounding Veronica as she'd hidden out in Javier's spare bedroom.

There was a baritone response and her eyes flew open. In the doorway was a dark-haired man with abuela...

Daniel. It was just her brother Daniel.

She closed her eyes and feigned sleep again, but Daniel had known her for too long. "Wake up, kiddo," he said, his weight making one side of her twin bed sag. "I'm here to check on you. Everyone's worried."

Not everyone. Not Lucas.

He rubbed her arm. "Come on. I know you're faking. You could always fool Mom and Dad, even Javier and Alex, but you could never fool me."

It was true. Daniel, her quietest, most intellectual brother, had been the most observant and perceptive, even as a teenager. He could tell the difference between awake breathing and sleep breathing, a relaxed muscle and a tense one. Little wonder he'd become a doctor.

And little use in trying to fool him now. "Okay, I'm awake," she admitted, opening her red, sore eyes and squinting against the daylight. "How's Belo? And how are the boys?"

"Belo's fine. He has a good visiting nurse, and Abuela has been checking in on him every day."

"Has Lucas?" The words were out before she could stop them. "Been checking in, I mean."

The side of Daniel's mouth twisted, and he took her hand

and squeezed it. "Yes. He checks in every day, according to Abuela."

"Does he... " Her throat tightened, and she coughed to cover it. "Does he ask about me?"

Daniel drew in a deep breath and let it out in a sigh. "Abuela didn't mention it, if he does. I'm sorry, Ronnie."

She nodded, swallowing. Of course he didn't check on her. His wife probably didn't allow it.

He probably didn't want to. "He's getting back together with his wife," she choked out.

"His *wife?*" Daniel stared at her. "He's married?" The last word came out like a gunshot. "And he let you get that close? Man, if I get my hands on him—"

"No, no, it's not like that. He's divorced, she left him because she couldn't deal with his illness, but apparently..." She paused. "Apparently she changed her mind."

Daniel let out a sound like a growl. "I'm sorry," he said again. "I wish there were something I could do to make you feel better. All I can say is... you *will* feel better. Not today, and not tomorrow, but someday." His words were kind, and so were his eyes.

"Thank you." If anyone was qualified to make such a statement, it was Daniel. He'd lost his wife, and later learned awful lies she'd told him. For a few years, he'd been a depressed hermit.

"I found love again," he said, "and maybe—"

"Don't," she said. "Just don't even... I know you mean well, but I can't think about that."

"Sure." He took her hands and pulled her the rest of the way into a sitting position. "For now, I need you to get up and come downstairs."

"No, I can't. Not yet."

"Yes, you can. You need to eat something. Your only choice is whether to take a shower first."

Well, she couldn't go downstairs without taking a shower, could she? And then once she was in Javier's bright kitchen, eating a plate of huevos rancheros, she started to notice all the life around her. Nora edged up and asked her how she was doing, and then immediately went into a long complicated story about a boy in her Algebra Two class. Daniel drove to El Corazon to pick up Roscoe and Tyrone, who were temporarily staying with Alex and Patricia, but who needed a ride. For whatever reason, he asked Veronica if she wanted to go along; she didn't, not really, but she also didn't have anything else to do, so she rode along. The boys were full of stories about their night at the restaurant, and seemed more glad to see her than worried about her state of mind or even about Lucas.

Teenagers—bless them in their self-absorption and their energy. It was hard to stay turned inward and depressed around them. And then, out at Alex's place, Bear the Golden Doodle came loping out to greet her joyously, lapping her face and nearly knocking her down, and his kind, foolish face made her laugh.

She didn't *want* to be depressed. She wanted life to go on, here in Arcadia Valley with her brothers and her abuela and all her friends from church and prayer group and El Corazon. Maybe she was overdependent on her brothers, sure, but in this situation, what would she have done without them? What would anyone do, all alone?

And she'd been wanting to throw away that love and strength because... why? Because she had something to prove?

Lucas's departure had knocked that desire right out of her.

Her brothers didn't urge her to talk a lot about what she was feeling. They just got her occupied with the teenagers and the restaurant and Abuela. Her own feeling of obligation made her check in on Belo. And then there were the emails she received, related to Lucas's research and business. Most of them went directly to him, but a few sources got in touch with her about interviews or research questions.

After a week, she had enough minor notes and messages that she needed to pass off to Lucas. She sent him an impersonal email, explaining each situation and asking how he wanted her to follow up.

The answer came back, terse and equally impersonal: no need to follow up, I'll take it from here.

There was something fishy about the whole situation. Everyone pitied Veronica and skirted the topic of Lucas, but she didn't feel pitiful. She felt angry.

Angry enough that, the morning after that impersonal email from Lucas, she visited Belo, closed the door behind her, and stood beside his bed, her hands on her hips. "Where is Lucas?"

He raised his bristly, salt-and-pepper eyebrows. "It is not my place to say."

"It wasn't his place to take off like that, leave us all behind so he could fight his battles alone, but he did."

"He did," Belo admitted, "but he is receiving good medical care. The best in the country, so it was the right decision."

"Was it the right decision for him to go back to his wife?" she asked, but before Belo could answer, there was a knock at the door and then Veronica's grandmother walked in. She was obviously as surprised to see Veronica as Veronica was to see her.

"I'm just checking on El Señor," Abuela said quickly, a flush rising to her cheeks.

Veronica studied her skeptically. What had been going on while she'd been occupied with Lucas and then with her own hurt feelings? "I'd like the chance to check on Lucas," she said, "but Belo won't tell me where he is."

"Lucas could tell you himself if he wanted you to know." Belo picked at his blanket.

Abuela gave Belo a light smack on the arm. "That is no kind

of answer. These young people don't know what they are doing, and need some help."

"I told him I wouldn't let anyone from Arcadia Valley know his whereabouts."

"Tell me this, Belo," Veronica said. "Is his wife taking care of him, such that none of us need to worry? Because if that's the case, I'll back off."

Belo looked blank. "His *wife?*"

"Yes," Veronica said impatiently. "He said he was getting back together with his wife."

"If he got back with that Tara, hell has frozen over," Belo said, "and I'll write down his address for you right now. He needs to be somewhere else than in that woman's clutches."

"You will?" Veronica was so excited that she forgot to be upset—although she *was* surprised that Belo knew Lucas's Tara, even if he didn't know they were married. Grandfathers always knew. "Abuela, will you cover for me? I have to go see him. Don't tell the boys. Tell them I... went to see an old school friend."

"I will not lie for you, my child," she said. "You will have to tell them yourself. But I have every confidence that you can."

Veronica looked at her grandmother. "You know what? You're absolutely right." She picked up the piece of paper Belo had printed out for her and made sure she could read it. Then she spun, hugged Abuela, and headed out the door to confront her brothers.

15

Did they get it all?

Through the anesthesia-induced fog in his brain, Lucas asked each nurse who visited his room to tell him how his surgery had gone. They'd all smiled politely and referred him to his surgeon, who'd had to go directly into another emergency surgery, but who would be in to visit just as soon as possible.

Their eyes held some kind of worry, and Lucas couldn't tell whether the problem was that the surgery had gone badly or that he didn't have anyone on his contact list. He'd taken a taxi to the hospital this morning, unwilling to walk the mile through downtown streets in the pre-dawn darkness. Getting mugged on the day of his tumor reduction surgery would be an idiot's move.

Reduction, or removal? The surgeon had given him fifty-fifty odds, had warned that even with full removal, there was a course of prophylactic chemo that would need to be done.

How he'd manage any of it alone, he didn't know. He only knew he couldn't burden Belo with it, or God forbid, Veronica. His few friends in Pittsburgh were more like acquaintances, not people who'd cook him chicken soup or hold the basin while he vomited.

He supposed that he'd run through all his money for skilled nursing care, and when that ran out, go into some nursing home run by the state. An inglorious end to a life that hadn't turned out at all the way Lucas had wanted.

He closed his eyes against the white walls and shiny machinery around him and took slow, deep breaths. It wasn't the end. He'd been reading his Bible faithfully, and some pretty heavy theological books as well. And yeah, it was a battlefield conversion, or at least a deepening of his faith.

In addition to the healing verses, he'd taken to studying the ones about going through hard times. Suffering produced endurance—check. Give thanks for all things—check. I can do all things through Christ—check.

There was a mansion prepared for him in heaven—double, triple check.

So maybe this experience wasn't so much about his health, but about his soul. Learning to be grateful for everything, for the up-to-the-minute medical care and the insurance that gave him access to it; for the love and caring in Belo's voice over the phone every day; for the sun slanting through the hospital windows and the kindness of a volunteer who refreshed his ice water.

Or the pastor who'd been visiting daily, who now swept in wearing jeans and a t-shirt, long-haired and bearded with a cross necklace, looking like an aging hippie. Jerome came right to the bed and smiled down at Lucas, putting a hand on his shoulder, carefully to avoid IVs and wires. "You look good for having just been under the knife, my man. How'd it go?"

"I feel like a truck hit me," Lucas admitted. His back and shoulder starting to hurt, which meant the anesthesia was wearing off. He was also feeling a little less loopy. And a little more anxious about what had happened while he'd been out. "They didn't tell you anything, did they?" he asked Jerome.

"No. I know nothing. When's the surgeon going to debrief you?"

"Anytime now." Lucas blew out a breath. "Waiting stinks."

Jerome didn't come out with some reproving comment about how Lucas should rely on God, and he appreciated that. Because yeah, Lucas was relying on God as best he could, but he wasn't superhuman. His worries and fears hadn't gone away.

"Mind if I stick around for a few?"

"That would be great." He held out the television remote.

"ESPN or the soaps?" Jerome asked with a grin. They'd only known each other a few days, but they both enjoyed baseball. And they'd discovered a mutual addiction to daytime TV.

"I'm thinking baseball," Lucas said, because he wanted to be able to talk to Jerome. Get a few answers about things the Bible said. The fact that Jerome didn't push it on him, that he was willing to just hang out and talk sports, made Lucas more comfortable discussing the God stuff. He didn't feel like Jerome would go in for the kill, try to make Lucas another notch in his "sinners saved" belt.

They watched the game for a few minutes, and Lucas endured a couple more rounds of checks by the nurses.

He turned to Jerome. "How do other people handle it?" he asked. "How do they deal with a bad diagnosis without freaking out or breaking down?" He didn't really mean "bad," he meant terminal. But he didn't even want to say the word.

Jerome shook his head. "I've seen it all, man," he said. "Some do break down. In fact, most people do at some point. It's normal."

"How do they pick themselves back up and go on?"

Jerome looked out the window for a minute and then turned to focus on Lucas, his dark eyes intent. "What do you have to live for?"

Lucas hadn't expected that question. "Um.... I don't know.

My work? My grandfather?" *Veronica?* He added inside his head but didn't say.

"What about your work makes you want to live for it?"

Lucas frowned. "When I was a war correspondent, it was important to get the word out about some things happening in the world. Still is important now that I'm covering developments in science and health. My articles, and I hope my book, they're to help people."

"Bingo." Jerome smiled at him. "That's a part of what you hold onto. You want to do a little more of that before you leave this earth."

Lucas nodded, slowly. He'd dearly love to finish the book on eating for cancer health. If it could keep someone from being here in his shoes, it would be worth it.

Thinking about the book made him think about the email he'd gotten from Veronica a few days ago. She'd been all business, but responsible, conveying information and offering to handle whatever he couldn't handle himself. That was Veronica, good to the core.

And if this was it, if this was how things were going to end, then he didn't want to leave things the way they were with Veronica. With abandonment and a lie. He'd done it for her own good, sure, but the result was hurtful.

"There's something I need to explain to someone," he said to Jerome. "That's not exactly a thing to live for, but it's a loose end I'd like to tie up."

"With your grandfather?" Jerome asked.

Lucas shook his head. "With Belo, I'm good. Well, I'd like to see him one time again, but there aren't loose ends. I've said what I needed to say."

"Sounds like you've got some work to do, my friend." Jerome stood up. "I'm praying for your full recovery. But even if that's the case, our time on this earth is short. You've just been put into a position to consider the long term, how you want to go out. Don't forget it, whatever happens."

"Thanks, man. And thanks for reminding me what really matters." He held up his Bible. Because that was the key thing, whether or not he got to accomplish everything he wanted to accomplish. He felt that peace of being right with God.

After Jerome left, Lucas muted the game so he could think. Think about his work. Think about Veronica.

There was a sound outside his door that made him jump a little, and he realized that he'd stopped obsessing and worrying about the surgeon's information. Jerome had helped to put it all in context. Everyone was a terminal case.

Still... Yeah. He wanted to know.

The door opened and he looked up, expecting another nurse but hoping for the doctor.

Instead, there was Veronica.

16

Veronica was so busy rehearsing what she'd say to Lucas that she didn't, at first, process the fact that she was in the room alone with him.

You were a jerk to walk out like that.

If you're choosing her over me at least have the decency to tell me why.

I think you ran out of fear.

We deserve a chance.

You really hurt me but I love you and I want to help you through this.

She was so busy mumbling to herself that his voice, low and scratchier than usual, was a shock.

"Veronica."

She looked across the room to the bed and saw him. Pale and wan, his eyes sunken, his normally-short hair shaven.

He looked terrible, and she'd never loved anyone so much in her life.

She wanted to run to him, to embrace him, to try to help, but something wouldn't let her do that—God, or wisdom, or fear, she wasn't sure which.

"Lucas?" She pushed the door a little further open. "Can I come in?"

He nodded once, and she made her way to the chair beside his bed. All of her planned conversation starters went out the window, right along with her anger and hurt.

Now she could see the bandage extending from his neck to his shoulder. She reached out and took his hand. It was cold. So cold. "Are you okay?"

A faint smile tugged at the corner of his mouth. "Yeah. Despite appearances to the contrary."

"They shaved your head."

He shook his head. "I've been visiting the kids' cancer ward. A lot of them are bald so..."

So he'd shaved his head in solidarity. The sweetness of that, in the midst of his own trouble, made Veronica's chest ache.

"Lucas, I want you to know—" she began.

But he raised a hand to silence her. "I did wrong to you. I need to tell you that I'm sorry. I lied."

"About what?"

"About Tara," he said. "I didn't go back to her. I don't even know where she is."

"Then why—"

"Because it would be a huge mistake for you to get involved with me, especially given all this, and that was my coward's way of pushing you away."

"You've got that right." The voice from the hospital door made them both jolt in surprise, and then Javier came striding in. "Lucas, man, you look like something the cat dragged in. And Veronica, you shouldn't even be here."

"Javier!" She stood and faced him, gripping his upper arms. "What are you doing here? Is everything okay at home?" But even as she asked the question, she processed what he'd done and said. "Wait a minute. Did you follow me here?"

"Regardless, he's right," Lucas said. "I agree 100%. You need to start your life without me, and all my issues, as a liability around your neck."

Heat rushed into Veronica's face and her heart started pounding triple time. She let go of Javier and took a giant step back. "You two! You don't get to make my decisions for me. When will you realize that and stop wasting your time?"

"Now, Ronnie. Don't get yourself all worked up. It's not important how I got here. What's important is that you don't make a big mistake."

Hands on hips, she glared at her older brother, ready to yell her rage at him. Then she glanced over at Lucas, like he was going to help her.

But no. Neither of those responses would do any good when what she really needed to do was to see herself as their equal and act that way.

Maybe she even knew a little more than either man. Because they were looking at logic, and looking at her as someone who needed protection.

She was pretty clear on the fact that the heart had more wisdom than the mind in this case. And that she didn't need nearly as much protection, right now, as Lucas did.

"Guys," she said, perching on the edge of Lucas's bed. She held out one hand to him and another to Javier, drawing her brother to sit in the chair beside Lucas's bed. "I actually think that worrying about me is a little misplaced right now." She looked hard at Javier. "We need to help Lucas, because that's what Quintanas do. We help our friends."

Javier had been opening his mouth to speak, but her words silenced him.

She turned to Lucas. "I know you've been independent," she said. "And I know you've been hurt by someone who was supposed to help you, and didn't." The fact that he hadn't reunited with his wife fluttered like a joyous butterfly in her chest. "But you're from Arcadia Valley, and the people there want to help you. It's great if you came here for surgery because they're the best, but for recovery, we want you back home."

"But—"

She held up a hand and got a dizzying, satisfying feeling of power. Why hadn't she been speaking up to her brothers, to men, forever? It felt wonderful.

But of course, this was different. This wasn't arguing about whether she should wear a particular dress or stay out late at the Legion. This was about something truly important, life and death. This was about caring for someone who needed it.

"Lucas," she said. "Don't you know that people *want* to help you? That they feel worse if you shut them out?"

There was a tap on the door, and then a white-coated man carrying a clipboard walked in. He blinked when he saw Javier and Veronica. "So you *do* have some family in the area."

"Friends," Lucas said, and introduced them. "Do you have news for me, Doc?"

"I do," he said, "and the question is whether you want to hear it in private or with your friends here."

Veronica's heart was pounding, her palms sweaty. Partly because of what the doctor might say, and partly wondering whether Lucas was going to shut them out.

Lucas looked from Veronica to Javier and back again. "If you're up for it," he said, "I'd like to have you stay."

"Good." The doctor came and sat on the other side of the bed near Lucas's feet. "You, Mr. Ruiz, are a very strong man. And I'm guardedly optimistic."

Lucas tilted his head to one side, his eyes narrowing. "Why optimistic and why guardedly?"

Dr. Stone nodded. "I'm optimistic because, to the best of my knowledge, observation, and experience, we were able to remove the entire tumor."

Veronica let out a startled scream and then covered her mouth, embarrassed. But Javier was pumping his fist in the air and Lucas grinned broadly.

"That's terrific news," he said. "I don't feel too bad for all that."

"That's what I meant when I said you were strong," the doctor said. "Your blood markers are excellent. Cholesterol, inflammation, all of it's better than with most patients I see."

Veronica couldn't help it; she fist-bumped Lucas. "All those Arcadia Valley vegetables," she said.

"And good muscle tone, too."

That's for sure. Veronica glanced at Lucas's muscular arms, revealed in his hospital gown, and felt her cheeks grow warm.

"So all of that is good," the doctor continued, "but I don't want to give the false impression that you're out of the woods. Cancer's a funny beast, and it can be hiding places we can't see, even with the best of instruments. Particularly when the spine is involved. That's why I'm going to recommend a course of prophylactic chemo."

Lucas blew out a sigh and rubbed a hand over his shaved head. "Good thing I don't have much hair to lose," he said.

Veronica looked at him quickly, trying to see whether his joke was hiding emotional upset, but it didn't appear to be. Lucas seemed resigned and his eyes were calm. "Does he need to do the chemo here, doctor?" she asked.

"Not at all," he said. "I'm accustomed to collaborating with doctors from all over the country."

"We're in the sticks," Javier said. "Arcadia Valley, Idaho."

"Near Twin Falls? I know some good people there."

Veronica blew out a breath. This was starting to look like a

God thing, but she didn't know whether Lucas's heart was in it or not. Nor if, should he come back to Arcadia Valley, he'd want her to be involved in his care. Maybe it would just be about coming home to his grandfather.

The doctor talked over a few more details with Lucas and then left, promising to return the next day. If Lucas was doing well, he could go home.

After he left, Javier stood. "I feel a little bit like a fool," he said, "for flying out here off the handle."

"You're kind of known for that," Veronica teased. It was common knowledge in Arcadia Valley that Javier had chased after Molly, when she'd suddenly left town during their high school romance. It hadn't ended well when they were teenagers, but they'd never stopped loving each other and finally, they were enjoying the happiness they deserved.

Would she and Lucas have any chance of that? She glanced over at him to see that he was studying her, a cryptic expression on his face. Her stomach turned over.

"Dude," Lucas said to Javier, "thanks for coming out, even though I know it wasn't to see me."

"It wasn't," Javier admitted. "It was to take care of my little sister, but I'm starting to realize she doesn't need that anymore."

His humble words brought tears to Veronica's eyes, and she stood and gave him a big hug. "You'll always be my big brother, and you can always *try* to boss me," she said.

Javier squeezed her tightly, then let her go, resting his hands on her shoulders and looking into her eyes. "You know I'm here for you the moment you need me," he said. Then he let her go and turned to Lucas. "And you, man. Work on getting better. Come home to the Valley and we'll help you." He leaned down and gave Lucas an awkward man-hug, then straightened. "And if you cause her to cry even one tear, you're a dead man."

"Understood. Thanks, man."

They both watched Javier walk out the door.

And then it was just the two of them, in the hospital room, with a world of questions between them.

17

"What is that fool grandson of mine doing now?" Belo asked Veronica as she plumped his pillows and poured him a fresh glass of water.

"He's not resting like he's supposed to be. But *you* need to worry about yourself." Belo had gotten a bad cold and the doctor was being careful about it, so Veronica had two invalids on her hands.

Only Lucas wasn't an invalid, not really.

So that couldn't be the excuse for why he'd distanced himself from her.

She was turning to leave when Belo pulled at her sleeve, spinning her back around. "You need to make sure to take care of yourself, too, young lady," he said.

"I do." Veronica dismissed that as more male overprotection.

But Belo kept ahold of her sleeve. "I hope that you are going to church and seeing your friends, talking this through."

"I am," she repeated, but when she looked into the old man's penetrating eyes, her pretend strength wooshed out of her. She sank down onto the side of his bed. "I'm talking to everyone but Lucas about it."

After he'd gotten his good news and had it out with his doctor, her, and Javier, she'd seen he was exhausted. So they'd had to postpone any sort of deep or meaningful discussion. And then when she'd returned to the hospital the next day, the place had been busy and crazy, not least in Lucas's room. The doctor had been giving dismissal instructions, and the nurse had been administering medications, and the social worker had been helping him make plans to fly home and get parallel care in Twin Falls.

He was to start his chemo as soon as he'd healed a little more, so he was working like crazy on his book, determined to make a lot of progress while he still had the strength. Veronica had been helping him with that, but there was no time for any discussion of their personal lives.

It was driving her crazy. But she didn't want to push too hard, because she dreaded hearing him say that he wanted to be just friends, or that she was too young to be with him, or that he'd had a change of heart.

Belo patted her hand. "You may need to lead the way," he said. "We men are not the best at talking things through. Sometimes, it takes a woman to get us to see the truth."

"You mean macho men like you and Lucas need a woman?" She squeezed his hand.

His eyes crinkled at the corners. "That's our biggest secret," he said.

"Is it true of you and *mi abuela*?"

He waved a hand. "This, I prefer not to discuss. Did you say you had things to do downstairs?"

She laughed at him and wandered downstairs, half hoping, half fearing to see Lucas. But instead, there was Tyrone, kneeling on the front porch in the warming spring sunshine. "Question for you," he said as soon as she came to the door.

"What is it?" she asked, and then she saw why he was kneeling. There was a mama dog on her side, and two puppies with another about to come, from the looks of things. She was giving birth on bare floorboards. "Tyrone! Why didn't you call me? What are we going to do?"

Before she could even make an attempt to help, Roscoe came rushing out of the house with a big armload of towels. Thick, fluffy, monogrammed towels, right from the dryer. Veronica winced, wondering what Lucas would say about the expense, then shrugged and helped Roscoe spread the towels in front of the dog. She seemed to understand, and nudged the puppies onto the new, comfortable bed. Then the two boys wiggled and jiggled the dog and the towels until they were under the mama as well.

The dog whimpered, her muscles tensing, and soon there was another pup. The boys watched with mingled fascination and horror as the mama dog cleaned off the tiny creature.

"Do you think that's all?" Veronica asked doubtfully.

"I don't know. I'm looking it up." Roscoe was studying his phone. "I think if she has another one, it'll be within the next half hour or so. Also, if we can touch her stomach we might get an idea."

"Should we call the vet?"

"No money," Tyrone said.

"Lucas has money. I have money. I'll put in a call to Dr. Hill." She did, and explained the situation.

"Is he coming over?" Roscoe asked.

"After work tonight. He said the dog is acting normal and that it sounds like everything is fine. Where'd the dog come from?"

"My folks," Tyrone said matter-of-factly. "They weren't taking good care of her, and they were gonna drown the pups when they came, so him and me—" He nodded at Roscoe. "We did a rescue."

"That's... good," Veronica said doubtfully. "But did you ask Lucas or Belo whether you can keep a dog here?"

"They did not." Lucas came around the corner of the house, wearing work boots and jeans.

Before she could think better of it, she rose and hurried to him. "What are you *doing?*"

"Putting in that garden," he said.

"But you shouldn't be working that hard!"

"I'll tell you about it," he said, "If you'll come on back and see. Guys, is the dog situation under control?"

"You *knew* about this?" Veronica stared at him. "And yet you didn't stick around?"

"The boys were handling it." He looked more closely at the dog as Tyrone and Roscoe puffed with pride. "Everything okay here?"

"Yeah," Tyrone said, eyeing him, "but only if we can have her stay here. She needs shelter and so do the pups."

"And I look like a sucker," he said. "Fine. They can stay."

"Told you," Tyrone said smugly to Roscoe.

Even the dog, glancing up and panting before going back to lick her pups, looked smug.

"Belo loves dogs," Lucas explained, "so he'll be the decision maker. Most likely, he'll want to keep the old girl and find homes for the puppies. And you boys will be in charge of that."

"We can do it," Roscoe said, fist-bumping Tyrone. "We'll give 'em to the cutest girls in town."

"Sounds like a plan. Come on," Lucas said, putting an arm around her and guiding her toward the back of the house. "You've gotta see."

His closeness made her heart pound faster. "Okay," she said, wishing she could think of something intelligent to say.

He brought her to the edge of the earth he'd turned earlier.

"Check it out," he said, picking up a clump of dirt and crushing it in his hand. "Good soil."

Where was he going with this? She knelt beside him and nodded. "We're known for it here in the valley."

"Right. But sometimes," he said, "it takes a little more understanding before we know how to plant something and make it grow." He tugged for her to look more closely at one corner of the garden, where tiny green shoots were starting to emerge.

"You planted something before you went back east!"

"Uh-huh. Sugar snap peas, and they'll be delicious when they start to bear fruit." He turned and looked right into her eyes. "Are you going to be around?"

"What do you mean?"

"When the harvest comes," he explained. His eyes never left hers.

"I... don't know." The way he was looking at her made her breathless. "I've decided I don't want to leave Arcadia Valley, but I don't know whether I'll have to go to Twin Falls to find work, or..."

"Or stay here with me?" He paused, then added, "As my website manager and research assistant and... as my wife?"

"*What?*" She sank the rest of the way onto the ground, not sure if she'd just heard what she thought she'd heard.

He put a hand in his pocket and pulled out a box. Then he turned to face her, still kneeling.

If this wasn't a proposal, she'd die. *Was* it a proposal? Her breath was coming so fast she thought she might pass out.

"Veronica," he said, "I know how I feel, and I know a lot more now about what's important. And I want to marry you."

She stared at his eyes, not sure if he was serious, unable to believe it.

"You're the most beautiful, caring, fun woman I've ever known," he said. "I think I've been in love with you from the moment I came back to town and saw you at El Corazon, surrounded by your brothers. I thought it might be just physical attraction—and it is that—but it's so much more."

Her face heated and she glanced away, then looked back into his eyes, so earnest and sincere.

"I don't want you to answer now," he said, sinking down to sit on one hip and tugging at her until she was sitting in front of him. He pulled her back against his shoulder and wrapped his arms around her. He inhaled deeply and kissed her ear, and chills ran through her body.

Then he nudged the box into her hand. "I want to give this to you, but it's not a ring. That comes later, if you decide we can pursue this thing."

"Then what is this?" She opened the box and found a green pouch inside. "Should I open it?"

"Please do." His breath was warm against her neck.

Slowly, she opened the pouch and drew out a shining silver necklace, embedded with turquoise and rose quartz, so gorgeous that she gasped. "It's an antique, Lucas. Where did you get it?"

"From Belo. My grandmother and my mother wore it. It's for my future wife."

She could barely breathe. "I... I don't—"

"It'll be hard," he interrupted. "I got a good report from my doctor, but you know how iffy that can be. Especially with cancer. And it's a sure thing that I'll be wiped out by the chemo."

"Lucas—"

"It would be totally understandable if you didn't want to do it. It's a big risk for you, and there are lots of other less complicated men who would be thrilled to call you their girlfriend. Or their wife. I don't expect you to agree, I really don't. I just felt like I had to go for it, to go for what I really want and ask you, because I'd be kicking myself for the rest of my life if I didn't at least try."

"Lucas—"

"I shouldn't even be asking you," he said. "I did get Javier's okay, but—"

"You *what?*"

"I had to ask him, Veronica. He's your eldest brother. I wouldn't want to encourage you to do anything that went against his wishes and beliefs."

She let her head sink down into her hands. "Unbelievable."

He leaned forward. "What's unbelievable?" he asked, his breath warm against her ear.

"Unbelievable that I'm actually considering saying yes," she said.

His arms froze around her, then tightened. "You *are?* With all my faults, someone like you, who could have any man she wanted, would consider..." And then he let go of her and scooted away and stood. When she turned, he had his back to her and was looking across the fields.

His shoulders shook, just a little.

He was *crying.*

Her heart nearly burst with love for this amazing, annoying man who was traditional enough to seek her brother's permission to propose, and yet in touch enough with his feelings to cry. She rose to her feet and came up behind him and wrapped him in her arms.

"Lucas," she whispered.

"Yeah?" He was still looking straight ahead, and she reached around to wipe the tears off his cheeks with the backs of her hands. Of course, she was crying too, and she wiped her own eyes so that their tears mingled.

As their laughter and tears would mingle until the end of their days. "My answer is yes," she said.

EPILOGUE

One year later, almost to the day, Lucas stood at the front of the church and waited for Veronica to walk down the aisle to him.

His heart was full.

Tyrone and Roscoe were his attendants, both looking grown in tuxedos. They'd both been accepted into the University of Idaho and would soon head off there as roommates. Tyrone intended to major in art, to everyone's surprise. And Roscoe had decided to go into nursing, after his experience helping his mother and then Lucas.

Abuela and Belo sat in the front row, because they'd beaten Veronica and Lucas to the punch and married at Christmastime. "At our age, we don't dare wait," Belo had explained, and so he and Veronica had gladly stood up for them at their small wedding.

Lucas looked at the cross on the altar and his eyes filled with tears. Chemo had been difficult, but he'd survived and was doing well. His hair was even starting to come back, although he'd elected to continue wearing it almost shaved.

He had to thank God for everything, even the cancer that

had brought him back to Arcadia Valley and taught him what was important, taught him to value his family and to value Veronica. They hoped to foster teen boys, having both found such joy in helping to launch Tyrone and Lucas.

It wasn't the typical family, and he still had misgivings about Veronica committing to a life that was almost certainly not going to allow her to have a child of her own.

She said it didn't matter, and he believed her. It was just that she'd be such a wonderful mother.

The music changed and he turned to see Nora and little Mimi, Alex and Patricia's little girl, coming down the aisle. Mimi was scattering flowers, coached by Nora, who looked lovely and grown up in a rose-colored dress.

And then Veronica appeared at the back of the church on Javier's arm, and his breath caught.

How had he gotten so lucky, so blessed, to have this woman for a wife?

Her hair hung long and loose beneath the white hat she'd elected to wear, and her dress was simple and modest, and he'd never seen anyone so beautiful in his life. But it wasn't just that she was pretty on the outside, although that was breathtaking. It was her soul, shining through. The sacrifices she made for others. The joy she brought to every person she encountered. The special, warm look she reserved only for him.

She and Javier reached the front of the church, and Lucas glanced away from Veronica to find his old friend to find him glaring at him. "You'd better take good care of her," Javier said in a voice audible enough that most of the congregation laughed.

Veronica laughed, too. And then she hugged Javier tight and kissed him on both cheeks. And finally, she turned to greet Lucas with eyes that swam with tears and love.

He held open his arms, he couldn't help it, and she walked right into them. They'd come close to losing each other and they were an unlikely couple, and he was stunned and thrilled that they could be together.

The minister cleared his throat. "If you don't mind, we have a wedding ceremony to perform here."

Everyone laughed again, and he and Veronica turned to stand in front of him and of their family and friends and say their vows.

Side by side, as they intended to go on for the rest of their lives.

THANK you for reading *Joy of My Heart*! If you want to find out a bit more about Lucas and Veronica's future, click here to read the very short (and surprising) second epilogue.

ARCADIA VALLEY ROMANCE

Six authors. Six series. One community.

Welcome to Arcadia Valley, Idaho, where a foodie culture and romance grow hand-in-hand. Join my friends and me as we release a book every month set in Arcadia Valley. You'll enjoy meeting old friends and making new ones as each of the six authors' books intertwine with the previous stories in this Christian romance series. Get started with *Romance Grows in Arcadia Valley* and follow along at ArcadiaValleyRomance.com to make sure you don't miss any installments!

AN

Arcadia Valley

ROMANCE

www.ArcadiaValleyRomance.com

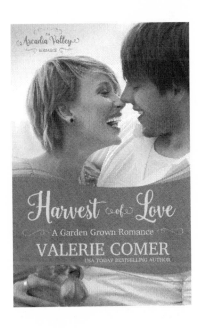

Hot on the heels of a failed relationship, Kenia Akers focuses on her bookstore along with granting her aging grandfather's desperate desire to get his hands in the dirt through a program at Grace Greenhouse. Reminding herself she's on the rebound isn't enough to keep her from falling for the hunky activities coordinator from Granddad's facility.

Zane Russell is amazed that the fun-loving, pretty bookstore owner is attracted to him, a guy who's not even in her league. As their relationship deepens, he avoids explaining why he seems allergic to books. Admitting his failures has never been a good move in the past.

Will they find a way to let openness, trust, and acceptance blossom into a harvest of love?

HARVEST OF LOVE

SNEAK PEEK

Kenia Akers shifted from one foot to the other at the back of the huge Bigby barn. She shouldn't have come to the benefit concert, but it had seemed even more lame to stay home on Valentine's Day when she'd been planning to attend for weeks. She'd dumped Jonah yesterday, but that was no reason to let her ticket go to waste. Maybe he'd use his for a bookmark... if he even had time to read since he was obviously pursuing Gloria Sinclair again. Jerk.

Wasn't it just Kenia's luck? Meet an adorable guy like Jonah Baxter on Christmas Eve, be wooed with whirlwind dates, only to discover he was still in love with someone else on February thirteenth?

She should've waited until after the concert to send him packing. At least she would have had one perfect Valentine's Day to remember. She'd have been here on the arm of one of the cutest, sweetest men she'd ever met instead of solo with half the town wondering about the demise of her short romance.

Kenia choked back a snort and tipped her chin up. Right. A perfect Valentine's Day, knowing he loved someone else?

On stage, Cole Anderson stood alone in the spotlight with his guitar as the elderly granny who'd sung the last song with him made her way down the steps and into the hushed audience. The spotlight divided, part of it coming to rest on Allie Bigby, the beneficiary of tonight's concert and silent auction. It sure stunk that Allie's lavender barn had burned down early Christmas morning. Then there'd been some glitch with her insurance. Arcadia Valley had pulled together to help raise the funds for rebuilding.

The mood shifted in the barn in that one long moment as Cole gazed down at Allie and Allie gazed back, her lips slightly parted and her eyes shining.

No way. There was only one thing that could be coming next, and it wasn't something Kenia wanted to witness. She pivoted for the door, only to discover she was blocked in by a wall of bodies. "Excuse me, please," she whispered once, twice, ten times as she edged toward the cold wintry night.

Cole's voice pushed into Kenia's consciousness. "Allie told me she loved me today, and I think you all know I love her, too."

Freedom beckoned from two people away. Kenia ducked between them, but one shifted and she connected with a hard elbow to her shoulder, spinning her sideways.

A warm hand caught her arm, steadying her, as startled eyes swung to meet hers. "I'm sorry. I didn't see you there."

Kenia stared into the gorgeous eyes of the man a few inches from her and tried to remember her words. His brown hair in need of a cut and his scruffy chin in need of a shave gave him a bad-boy image, unlike Jonah, Mr. Perfect.

On stage, Cole began singing a love song.

Immeasurably better than a proposal, but no doubt one was coming. This song was only a reprieve but, knowing Cole and Allie's history, he'd had years — decades — of unrequited love to pen at least twenty-five stanzas.

That didn't mean she should stand here like she'd been

struck by lightning staring at a total stranger until Cole's final strum.

"Excuse me, please." Too bad she couldn't muster anything other than a breathless whisper.

A grin crinkled his face and warmed those eyes just as the heat of his hand left her arm.

Kenia yanked her gaze away and pushed open the barn door. Outside, icy air chilled her heated cheeks as she dashed across the crowded parking area to her car. A motion sensor blinked a light into action, cutting the view of the smattering of stars that bravely attempted illumination of the dark night.

With shaking hands, Kenia stuffed the key in her ignition, started her Ford Fiesta, and drove away from Bigby Farm. Whew. At least she'd missed the proposal. Sure, she was happy for Allie. She'd known the woman since high school. If anyone deserved to find true love and happiness, it was Allie.

Only... why not Kenia? Why had she wasted six weeks dating a man who couldn't stop dreaming about another woman? There'd been niggles of doubt, but she'd ignored them. She'd known Jonah'd had a thing for Gloria Sinclair for several years, but it had never gone anywhere. Kenia hadn't thrown herself at him. He'd been the one to invite her to his brother's wedding. He'd been the one to hold her close while they danced, who'd kissed her, albeit briefly, at the stroke of midnight on New Year's. He'd been the one who'd invited her to his family dinners, cooked her amazing meals, and snuggled her while they watched movies.

She hadn't dreamed all that. He'd been the one pursuing her. Hadn't he?

Okay, maybe his kisses had lacked passion, but that had been welcome after Damian who'd groped her on their first and only date. Passion would build as their relationship developed and, one day, he'd ask her to marry him. She'd become Kenia Baxter. There'd be total fireworks by then.

Or not. She should've seen it coming. Should have, but hadn't. Not until yesterday when Gloria entered A Slice of Heaven, the bakery run by the Baxter family, and caught Kenia kissing Jonah. He'd been distracted. He'd made donuts for Gloria — expected her — and Kenia could tell he hoped she hadn't figured that out. He'd called Gloria when his sister had been rushed to the hospital to save the life of her unborn baby. Not Kenia. No, she found out accidentally, after the fact.

Having those blinders ripped off had been painful, but she had to hold her head up high in the community. Arcadia Valley was small, and everyone knew everyone else's business. Kenia managed Page Turners, her aunt's bookstore, so escaping town wasn't an option. The only salve she'd been able to muster had been breaking up with Jonah before he broke up with her.

She'd brought the basket of books and the Page Turners gift certificate out to the benefit concert as promised, ready to tell anyone who noticed she was alone that she'd called it off with Jonah. She hadn't expected to be required to witness Cole Anderson proposing to Allie Bigby.

That guy in the back of the barn. Who was he? Not a reader, or she'd have seen him in the bookstore... unless he was one of those who preferred e-books or bought his paperbacks online. She shuddered. Maybe he was a friend of Cole's from out of town, just visiting for the concert. Probably that was it. A better thought than him not being a reader or not supporting the local bookstore.

Kenia pulled into the parking spot in front of her small cottage. She'd never see him again. That was fine. She needed time for her broken heart to mend.

~

THE GUY on the stage crooned on and on, obviously besotted with the young woman in the other spotlight. She was kind of pretty, with her tousled brown hair falling to her shoulders, but not as pretty as the woman he'd elbowed as she dodged past.

Zane Russell glanced at his friend Quinn standing beside him. "Who was that?"

"The girl who left in such a hurry? Kenia Akers. Wonder what her problem was." Quinn shrugged. "She runs the bookstore downtown."

Bookstore. Zane should forget about her right this minute. Forget about her short but fiery orange hair, forget about the sadness in her eyes... had they been blue? Hard to tell in the dim light. "Married?" Man, had that really come out?

Quinn's eyebrows pulled together as he gave Zane his full attention for a minute. "Who are you talking about? Kenia? No, she's not married. I think she's dating someone, though. Last I heard, not that I keep track."

"It's Valentine's Day. If she were dating, she wouldn't have been sad and alone."

"So maybe they broke up." Quinn shrugged and faced the front, where the final guitar strums finally faded.

There was a silent auction spread out on tables across the back of the barn. Surely a local bookstore would have donated something to such a worthy cause. Zane wended his way through the standing guests, vaguely aware of the musician asking the woman to marry him. By the cheering of the crowd, she said yes.

Ah, there was a stack of books wrapped together with a band of brown paper on the back table. He didn't bother scanning the titles, just glanced at the bid sheet. Someone had bid $100. They were hardcovers. Probably worth that much or more on eBay. He scrawled $125 below it. Beside it was a listing for a $75 gift certificate with the same emblem as the paper by the books. The last bid was $80. He scribbled $100 on that one. Hopefully the engagement would keep people from coming to the back table to check their bids.

Wait, this was a stupid idea. He didn't need to spend money to find her store and introduce himself. Almost all the businesses in town were along Main Street or in that mini-mall where the bakery was. He could just stroll down the sidewalk and find the bookstore easily enough.

Russell, you're an idiot. You don't even read.

Yeah, well. Maybe he'd start.

The voice in his head burst out laughing. Okay, fine. It was unlikely. Anyway, Kenia Akers probably had other hobbies. She was around books all day at work, so she likely did other things in the evenings. Hiking, maybe. Biking. Kayaking. Of course, it was well below zero outside in mid-February, so he'd need other ideas to tide him through until warmer weather. He'd think of something.

A guy about Zane's age moved to the table closest to the door and tapped a wireless microphone. "Can I get everyone's attention, please? I'm Andrew Bigby, and I'd like to thank everyone for coming tonight and helping my sister's lavender business get back off the ground. Your generosity means a lot to our whole family. The silent auction has wrapped up, so let me just announce the lucky winners. If your name is called, please make your way to the item you bid on, and my wife, Layla, will accept your payment. Okay? Let's get going then."

Panic seized Zane's throat. Had he really bid on both the bookstore packages? And no one else was hurrying over to up the bid? *Come on, somebody.* His eyes scanned the crowd, but they all seemed content with whatever the outcome would be.

"The final bid on a bouquet from Blossoms by the Akers is one hundred eighty dollars. The bidder is Emerson Hadley. Thank you, Emerson and Blossoms by the Akers."

Andrew shifted to the next item. "The final bid on a three-day rafting trip is nine hundred fifty dollars. Thank you, Felipe Espinoza, for that great bid on a package by Snake River Tours."

A Latino man jogged to the back, pumping his fists, as a few people cheered.

"Well, that ought to be interesting," murmured Quinn from beside Zane. "He's a cop with five kids, all girls."

Zane tried for a chuckle, but it was hard.

Andrew picked up the next sheet. "The final bid on a seventy-five dollar gift certificate to Page Turners is one hundred dollars." He squinted at the paper. "Thank you, Zane Russell and to Page Turners for your donation. Wait, the next one is also from Page Turners for a set of six romance novels. Zane Russell, you're also the high bidder on this package with a bid of one hundred twenty-five dollars. Thank you."

An elbow caught the middle of Zane's back. "You bought a set of trashy romance novels?" Quinn chortled. "What were you thinking, man?"

Heat crept up Zane's cheeks. He should've taken a closer look. The bid sheet had been on top, but he hadn't even looked at the covers. He'd only been thinking about a chance to meet Kenia Akers. Well, he'd get that chance, times two. Although the books were right here, and once he'd paid for them, he'd take them home. No trip to a bookstore would be necessary. What an idiot.

With wooden legs he moved over to where Layla was accepting a check from the police officer. Hopefully she had a method of accepting charge cards, too. He hadn't exactly intended to spend anything tonight.

She shifted her attention to him with a bright smile. "Your name?"

"Uh. Zane. Zane Russell."

Layla grinned. "That will be two hundred twenty five dollars, Mr. Russell. You must be an avid reader."

Best not to answer that part. He pulled out his wallet. "Can you take Visa?"

"Sure." She pulled out a cell phone and attached a small device. "I can just slide the card right through here."

"Great." He waited for the transaction to be complete then tucked the gift certificate into his wallet along with the card. Hopefully the bookstore also stocked gift items. Didn't most of them?

Then he reached for the stack of books. Man, he couldn't believe he'd let temporary insanity rule.

"Oh, wow, I was counting on winning that bid." A young woman dragging a small child by the hand glanced at the books and shook her head with a smile. "The one on top just came in this week, hot off the press, but I hadn't made it down to Page Turners to buy a copy yet. I've been waiting to get into this series until all the books were out."

Zane thrust the pile toward her. "Here you go."

"What?" Her startled eyes met his. "No. You bought them."

"That's okay. Really. You can have them. Happy Valentine's Day or something." Romance novels for Valentine's. Sounded like a match made in heaven.

Her gaze lingered on the books then shifted back to him. "Are you sure? I'm happy to pay you for them."

"Absolutely certain. Enjoy."

"But your wife... or girlfriend..."

"I think she's probably read them, after all." It was only a little white lie. If he had a girlfriend like Kenia — crazy thought that had possessed him — she would have read them by now, right?

Zane pushed the pile at the woman until her hands came up

to accept the books. Then he nodded abruptly and edged his way out of the hot, crowded barn into the chilly parking area.

He should've come out here first, before doing something so stupid as bidding on a stack of books. If he'd thought at all, which he hadn't, he'd have assumed they were mysteries or maybe science fiction. Thrillers, maybe. But romance novels?

If he were a reader, he would've kept them. Maybe found some ideas on how to win a woman over. But, yeah, he wasn't a reader.

OTHER TITLES IN THE SERIES

Interested in Lee's Sacred Bond series or her romances from Love Inspired? Visit her website to check out all her books. And if you'd like, sign up for her newsletter and get a short novella, *Before the Bond*, free!

Fifteen years before the Sacred Bond, a college girl and a working-class veteran started to fall in love . . .

LEE TOBIN MCCLAIN

Before the Bond

Sign up for Lee's newsletter and download their story . . . for free!

ABOUT THE AUTHOR

Publishers' Weekly bestselling author Lee Tobin McClain read *Gone with the Wind* in the third grade and has been a hopeless romantic ever since. When she's not writing angst-filled love stories with happy endings, she's probably reading a mystery novel, driving around her gymnastics-obsessed teenage daughter, or playing with her rescue dog and cat. In her day job, Lee gets to encourage aspiring romance writers in Seton Hill University's low-residency MFA program.
Visit her website to join her mailing list and get a Sacred Bond pre-prequel story, *Before the Bond,* free!

Connect with Lee
www.leetobinmcclain.com

COPYRIGHT PAGE

Copyright © 2018 by Lee Tobin McClain.

All rights reserved. No part of this publication may be repro-
duced, distributed or transmitted in any form or by any means,
including photocopying, recording, or other electronic or
mechanical methods, without the prior writ-ten permission of
the publisher, except in the case of brief quotations embodied in
critical reviews and certain other noncommercial uses permitted
by copyright law. For permission requests, write to the publisher,
addressed "Attention: Permissions Coordinator," at the address
below.

tobin@setonhill.edu

www.leetobinmcclain.com

Publisher's Note: This is a work of fiction. Names, characters,
places, and incidents are a product of the author's imagination.
Locales and public names are sometimes used for atmospheric

purposes. Any resemblance to actual people, living or dead, or to businesses, companies, events, institutions, or locales is completely coincidental.

Joy of My Heart / Lee Tobin McClain. -- 1st ed. Copyright ©

Made in the USA
Middletown, DE
22 January 2022

59399922R00113